Acclaim for
Kinda Sorta American Dream:
Collected Stories

"With his timely debut collection, *Kinda Sorta American Dream*, Steve Karas announces himself as an exciting voice of immense breadth and literary talent. The masterful title story alone is worth the price of admission, but all of the fourteen stories here shimmer with compassion, intelligence, wit, and grace. From a social worker in a new high school to a Santa-in-training, a toy collector to a disaffected teen, Karas inhabits his wide array of characters with eerie accuracy. Filled with ache and longing, these keenly drawn portraits afford Karas a sharp look at the founding promise of our country, a bleak skewed shadow of its once bloated self, but not without a future of possibility or hope."

- Sara Lippmann, author of *Doll Palace*

"*Kinda Sorta American Dream* is a glittering gem, a buttery cookie, a lit firecracker, hissing—exactly what I look for in a short story collection! This is Americana in all its buzzing splendor—the reaching and breathing and believing and hope. [Karas'] writing is brilliantly tight even when his characters are restless and wandering. *Kinda Sorta American Dream* is observant and thoughtful, and I have no doubt this is his first of many books."

- Leesa Cross-Smith, author of *Every Kiss A War*

"*Kinda Sorta American Dream* presents a vivid tableau of survivalists and survivors, infidels and ghosts. Steve Karas sensitively captures the current moment through resonant characters caught between a tarnished past and an unknowable, uncertain future. A truly compassionate portrait of contemporary America."

- Shawn Syms, author of *Nothing Looks Familiar*

"Don't be fooled by the modesty of the words 'Kinda Sorta' in its title. This is a dream of a story collection full of diverse, well-fleshed characters whose struggles to make a life for themselves in both contemporary and futuristic versions of America—whether they be a Greek diner owner seeking to reclaim his lost youth via the quasi-reality of social media, an African-American cop contending with what it means to pledge full allegiance to the badge amid rampant cases of police brutality, or a Midwestern man seeking work as a provider of cuddles in a connection-starved 2030 society—stay with you like the remnants of nocturnal visions. Karas switches between these various voices with empathy and authenticity. He is a writer to watch."

- Apollo Papafrangou, author of *Wings of Wax*

"What Steve Karas so authoritatively illustrates in this far-reaching debut collection is that the journey to achieving the American Dream may take many paths, but it doesn't come without pain, fear or loss. Assuming it comes at all. And yet despite this, in Karas' empathic hands, this journey is still one filled with vivid characters, a sense of hope and the joy of discovering an author at the start of something new and wonderful."

- Ben Tanzer, author of *The New York Stories, Lost in Space* and *Orphans*

KINDA SORTA AMERICAN DREAM

COLLECTED STORIES

STEVE KARAS

TAILWINDS PRESS

Tailwinds Press
P.O. Box 2283, Radio City Station
New York, NY 10101-2283
www.tailwindspress.com

Published in the United States of America
ISBN: 978-0-9967175-0-2
1st ed. December 2015

In loving memory of my cousin, George

CONTENTS

Ain't Like the Movies 1

To Abdo, with Love 11

Sculpting Sand 23

Kinda Sorta American Dream 37

It Takes a Village 57

Hold On 107

The Uncounted 115

Sixteen Hundred Closest Friends 127

Red Clay 145

Kingdom Come 155

Toys in Closets 169

Blue 197

Catching Fire 207

Savior 209

KINDA SORTA AMERICAN DREAM

AIN'T LIKE THE MOVIES

I'm sitting at the kitchen table over a bowl of soggy oats, hives crawling up my neck, eyes watery and itchy. It's the cats; I'm deathly allergic. My mom brought home three last night.

"Cute, aren't they?" she says, wrapped in a white bathrobe swiped from a recent staycation with Rick at the Comfort Suites.

The Siamese brushes against my leg. I blow my nose into a napkin.

"Hey, who pissed in your cereal?"

"You're trying to kill me, aren't you, Mom?" I say.

"What? You've been talking about moving out. No way was I going to pass up the opportunity when I found these little lovies on Craigslist."

"I never said anything about moving out."

My parents divorced when I was twelve. I stayed with Mom. Rick is her first real boyfriend since. Until he came along, she never wanted me to leave her side, even discouraged me from going away to college. "What are you going to learn at some university that I can't teach you here?" But for the last eight months she's been dropping not-so-subtle hints. "Don't you want a steady girlfriend, Jeffrey? What girl is going to date a twenty-seven-year-old who still lives at home with his mom?"

The cats are circling me now, looking for handouts. "So where am I supposed to go?" I say. I sneeze on my cereal. "Where the hell am I supposed to go?"

My car's wipers can't keep up with the falling snow as I'm driving to work. The vents are blowing in cold air. This is my second tour with Blockbuster Video, the first being a decade ago. I'd wanted to go into film, direct movies, be the next James Cameron. I spent a semester commuting to Ivy Tech to study visual communications before getting kicked out for bad grades. Too much Xbox, too much pot. So the video giant was my next best move. I got the job through my old high school buddy, Chang, but was fired from that first go-around when I skipped work to audition for *Big Brother*. I've been with them for sixteen months now. I started as a CSR making $8.25 an hour, got promoted to Shift Leader before long. My sights are on Manager.

I pass the Colonial Park Apartment Complex. Sounds regal, looks shoddy. I could probably afford a place there, a place to call home, a place to lay my head. Or I could get myself a posh crib downtown, be a real Swinging Dick Willy. Man, I don't even know how to cook. I won't starve on my own, but there's a good chance I'll die young from eating frozen pizzas and Hot Pockets every day.

I walk into the store. My shoes drag in snow, my glasses fog. Dusty, the manager, greets me by habit. "Welcome to Blockbuster."

"What up, douche?" I say.

He pulls me aside. "Listen, I already told everyone else. The store's closing in two weeks. We're all going to be out of work."

"You're kidding me, right?"

"I wish I was. Lease is up. Company's not extending it."

"And they're not transferring us?"

"Nope, not even me. I'll be right there next to you in the unemployment line."

"Yeah, you're still in high school though, man. I'm a grownup. I need a job."

"Hey, I'm just the messenger, dude."

I want to pop the giant zit on Dusty's nose or give him a wedgie. I want to do something. My gaze shifts to the back wall, to "Jeff's Picks," and I breathe in deeply. *Caddyshack, Risky Business, Death Wish*. Classics. "Fuckin' Redbox," I mutter. "Fuckin' Netflix."

I'm packing what little I own. I can hear my mom and Rick giggling from the family room, watching some lame movie like *The Devil Wears Prada*. The cats keep meandering through my clutter, jumping on and off the bed, sticking their noses into boxes. I shoo them away, but they keep coming back. I want to rip my eyeballs out they itch so bad.

The cats have taken to me, especially the Siamese, because I'm the only one who bothers to feed them. It's like they think I'm their master or alpha male or pal, if cats even think like that. I've never been a cat fan. They're cold, aloof. I'm a dog person. When I get my own place one day, that's what I'm going to do—I'm going to get myself a dog. Maybe a golden retriever or a shepherd.

I stuff as many of my clothes as I can into a gym bag and pile the rest into a laundry basket. Before Rick, before the cats, my mom collected dolls. Antique dolls. Wax dolls and China dolls, German dolly-faced dolls. She spent thousands on them. Now they're all shoved into closets and under beds. The Siamese tugs one out by the arm from under my nightstand.

My mom comes to my room in that damn bathrobe and leans against the door frame. Her frosted blonde hair sits against a backdrop of dark roots and black eyebrows. Rick rolls up behind her, slurping down a carton of Neapolitan. "So what's the verdict?" Mom says. "Where's my boy headed, all grown up and ready to face the world?"

"I'm moving in with Dad."

Her jaw drops. "Oh, c'mon. No you're not. Please tell me you are not."

It's clear she wants me to stay now, subconscious memories of legendary courtroom battles surfacing. "I have no place else to go," I say. "He's willing to let me crash there until I can get on my feet."

My mom looks at Rick. He shrugs his shoulders. One of the cats is yanking at his dirty shoelace. I grab a stack of DVDs, toss them into the bag, and give it a zip.

My dad insists I call him Kevin now that I'm a grown man. So Kevin, like an idiot, leaves his computer on. I hop on to start doing some job hunting. He's logged into eHarmony and chatting with Tammy R. The Tammy whose profile I showed him. The Tammy who I told him I was sweet on. Two other browsers are opened to OkCupid and Indianapolis Singles. Yeah, he's been hitting on Yvette, Stephanie, and Laura G. too.

When Kevin let me move in a week ago, the agreement was that I would teach him the ropes of online dating. So I did. Now he's cock-blocking me, trying to chat up all the girls he knows I'm pursuing.

Kevin walks through the door in a winter hat and tracksuit, a fruit punch Gatorade in one hand and a pack of Marlboro Lights in the other. "You fart?" he says. "Fuckin' stinks in here."

Ever since he and Mom split, he thinks he's become a real player. He never once took us on a family vacation, not even to the Dunes. Now he takes all his little hookers on Caribbean cruises and 500-dollar-a-night ski excursions. He tans and takes kung fu lessons, thinks he can kick anyone's ass. For years, he's been harassing me about training with him. He says it'll teach me discipline and trim off my man boobs.

Kevin, see, doesn't really work. He inherited buildings and strip malls across the city owned by my grandfather. The buildings are paid off now. Kevin has people managing them, and he collects the rent. He lives in a pimped-out unit of a condo complex he owns.

"Why are you trying to steal my chicks, Kevin?" I say, nodding to the computer.

"Snooze you lose, son. That's life. You grab what you can when you can. I could've taught you that and more if you'd lived with me, but you had to stay with your mommy."

I don't say anything, not because I don't want to. I don't because if I tell him to go fuck himself and remind him how little he was there for me over the last fifteen years, he's liable to send me packing. Which would be fine if I had anyplace else to go.

I'm driving around town looking for "Now Hiring" signs. I'm desperate. I'm willing to take a job anywhere at this point, to start saving, begin my life. I should sign up for some online courses, finally work toward that elusive degree.

My phone rings. It's my buddy, Chang. We've lost touch lately, haven't connected as often as we'd like since he moved to L.A. Chang and I used to be tight. We'd make home movies together as kids, horror and war movies. We'd use fireworks and Halloween putty to construct fake fingers and severed limbs.

Chang fills me in on how things are going in La La Land. He's dyed his hair platinum blonde. He's now the Post-Production Coordinator—whatever that means exactly—for *American's Best Dance Crew*. Before that he was working on *The Sing-Off* and some other TV shows I've never heard of but impress me, nonetheless. The point is, Chang is making it. Chang is living the dream. My toes are freezing, my knuckles are dry, and I'm fantasizing about the California sun.

"Chang," I say, "I know this sounds crazy, but what do you think about me coming out there?"

"What do you mean, to live?"

"I don't know, maybe. Do you think I could crash at your place?"

"Dude, that would be awesome. Are you serious?"

"I think I am." I've never lived outside Indiana. Only been away from the great Hoosier State twice, for a family reunion in St. Louis and the 2002 Comic-Con Convention in Dallas. "You don't have any cats, do you?"

"Cats? No cats, man. Thinking about getting a Chihuahua, though. Everyone out here has a Chihuahua."

"I'm cool with Chihuahuas," I say, "I love Chihuahuas."

I'm packing. Again. My mom calls. She's in Vegas with Rick.

"Jeffrey? Hey, it's Mom. I have some great news. Ready? Rick and I got married last night. Jeff, can you hear me?"

"Yes, I can hear you."

"Rick and I got married last night!"

"What can I say, Mom? Congratulations."

"Look, we'll be home in a few days. Do me a favor, will you? Make sure to stop by and check on the cats."

"You left the cats alone. Nice, because they really can take care of themselves."

"What's that?"

I raise my voice. "I said, 'Nice, because the cats can really take care of themselves.'"

Mom giggles. It sounds like Rick is tickling her. "Okay, gotta let you go. We're about to go on a gondola ride at the Venetian." I hang up.

Kevin walks into the living room with two Bud Lights. I'm watching *Platoon* on his big screen. He sits next to me on the black leather couch.

"Jeff, I've got some good news I want to share with you." I don't bother turning off the TV, so Kevin shouts over the sound of grenades exploding. "I'm moving to Florida with Tammy." My Tammy, apparently.

"And how is that good news?"

"I know we've only been dating for a few weeks, but I'm crazy about her. She's a real firecracker. Good news for you is I'm leaving you this condo. I'm not even taking any of the furniture with me. Tammy wants to buy all new stuff out there."

"Okay."

"I can put this complex in your name too. If you help manage it, we can split the earnings fifty-fifty."

"Why would you do that?"

"We're cut from the same thread, son. Most kids have to work for what they get. You're lucky to have a successful dad who actually gives two shits about you."

I stare at the screen, trying to take it all in. It's the iconic Sergeant Elias death scene. Betrayed by his own comrade in arms. I look back at my dad, my flesh and blood, and take a swig of beer. "Go fuck yourself, Kevin."

Before I leave town, I stop at my mom's to check on the cats. The hallway of the apartment building smells unmistakably of cat shit. It gets worse as I approach Mom's door. I bury my nose into my coat. The neighbor, an old grizzly, hears me and pops her head out.

"What's going on?" she says. "Someone die in there? It's stunk since yesterday."

The cats are clawing at the door as I'm jiggling the key. When I open it, they try to squeeze past my legs and out into the free world. The apartment is like a crime scene. Lamps and chairs are knocked over. My mom's antique dolls are strewn across the floor, hair plugs torn from heads, legs and arms separated from sockets.

The old bat winces and covers her mouth. "Oh, Lord, you can't leave those helpless little angels alone like that. Your mom think she'd come home and see they'd raised themselves? We're not talking about Garfield here or Tom and Jerry. Life ain't like the movies."

"You got that right."

"I have a good mind to call the Humane Society."

"Go for it," I say.

The litter box is overflowing, the water and food bowls flipped over. I can feel my face begin to swell and a rash developing on my neck. The Siamese is staring up at me with its blue eyes and a, frankly, cute nose that looks like it's been dipped in black paint. He says "Meow," but I hear "Save me." I reach down to pet him and he doesn't resist. "It's okay, little buddy," I say. "It's going to be okay."

TO ABDO, WITH LOVE

My boyfriend, Abdo, lives in a country called Syria. He likes to play soccer and war games. He wants to become a doctor when he grows up. I'm supposed to be paying attention to Miss Clark at the board, learning how to express probabilities as decimals, but instead I'm staring at the laminated map pinned to the wall and daydreaming about Abdo.

Willy Finnegan, Amber Alert hair and freckles like land mines, turns in his seat and mouths to me, "I can't find my homework. You eat it?" I growl at him and look away. He hates me because I've won three Spelling Bees, because I get straight As when he can barely read.

Today is Abdo's birthday. We met as pen pals in the fourth grade. He's twelve now, which is hard to believe. Haven't heard from him since last year. My teacher said his school was blown up in the war, kids were forced to drop out, families given no choice but to leave their homes. Some of the jerks in my class like Willy jumped out of their seats when she told us, pumped their fists, got all excited about how cool it would be if our school got blown up too, if they could take a year off and play street football and videogames. Boys in this country are so immature.

I drew Abdo a birthday card, but don't have any place to send it. A three-layer cake with strawberries and buttercream frosting. A picture of him smiling, waving out the window of a big plane headed to America, his family in the windows behind him. I sign it, "To Abdo, with love—Stephie."

Dad is slouched in his brown recliner, socks kicked off, a beer bottle in his hand. My little brother, Paul, is at his feet playing with toy soldiers. Over the sizzle of onion and beef on the stovetop, the fan blowing, I hear the newscaster on TV say something about Syria. I look up from my Science worksheet on noble gases and the crown atop Queen Helium. My mom lifts her head from a cloud of smoke.

On the screen are videos of kids shaking on the dirt floor, a woman with a gray scarf covering her face spread out over concrete stairs, a line of kids on the ground, eyes shut and a blanket across them like they're having a slumber party. There are flies buzzing all around them. I hear words like "graphic" and "gruesome" and "horror," and I try spelling them to myself. "Do you think we're going to send troops?" Mom says. Her eyes are tearing, but I think it's from the onion.

Dad doesn't answer. He takes a swig of his beer. Paul is making explosion sounds with his mouth, marching a soldier over Dad's feet.

My dad is in the Army. We live on-base here at Fort Campbell. It looks a lot different than where Abdo is from. We have grass and rolling green hills. We have a bowling alley and a movie theater, baseball fields and a Southern buffet. My dad says the only difference between us and the rest of America is that we live behind a guarded fence, and if there ever was a civil war in this country we'd be the last place anyone would mess with.

Dad turns off the TV and comes into the kitchen. I'm scared one of the dead kids is Abdo but I tell myself not to think like that. That's what my mom would say when Dad was in Afghanistan and we would hear about another American soldier killed. Gunfights, roadside bombs, friendly fire. Don't think like that. I don't even know what Abdo looks like, but I bet I'd recognize him if I saw him.

As much as I don't want my dad to leave us again—for my mom to have to convince herself every day not to think like that—I know he's the only person in the world who can find Abdo for me. And so I feel awful, but there's a little part of me that hopes he gets deployed to Syria for just a bit.

We're running the mile in P.E. Around the soccer field, past the strike zone drawn in white chalk against the orange brick wall, past the American flag flapping on the pole. I'm jogging as hard as I can, but I'm still way behind everybody else. Willy Finnegan laps me.

"Move it, fat ass," he says.

"Shut up, jerk."

Our teacher is in the center circle, whistle hanging from her neck, playing with her phone. I've told on Willy before. The teachers never see him do anything though. Never catch him in the act.

I'm panting like our old yellow lab and concocting my plan which revolves around Lieutenant Colonel Robert Powell—my dad—recent commander of the second battalion, 327th Infantry in the 1st Brigade Combat Team, 101st Airborne Division. When I was ten years old, he spent a year in Afghanistan, Operation Enduring Freedom XI, the year I went through a serious bedwetting stint. Before that, he took me and Mom—pregnant at the time—to see *Happy Feet* a week before my sixth birthday, and then left for Iraq on a two-year tour. When he got back, Paul was a year and a half and jumping off the living room couch. I don't remember the first time Dad went to Afghanistan, but Mom tells me I would only sleep in bed with her and would hide behind her legs in public. She says it's impressive I have such an extensive vocabulary when I wouldn't even speak back then.

Everyone says I'm just like my dad. No quit in us. Go-getters. At home, my Spelling Bee trophies are displayed next to his medals—the Air Medal, the NATO Medal, the Army Commendation Medal for Valor.

So my plan is to make hundreds of flyers and have Dad pass them out to the locals in Damascus, where Abdo lives:

Do you know a boy named Abdo?
Birthdate: August 23, 2002
Hobbies: Soccer, War Games
Future Job: Doctor

I wish I had a picture of him. When Dad finds him, he'll give him my birthday card. Abdo will be overjoyed, and Dad will ask him to give me a letter in return. He'll find Abdo's parents and see if they have any family in the United States, if they would like to flee to this country where we have schools that are open and Southern buffets. Dad may need a translator.

My teacher is at the end line, staring at her stopwatch. "C'mon, Stephie, finish strong," she says. Everybody is already done, standing behind her with hands over their heads or pressed against their bent knees. Willy is surrounded by his other jerk friends, all pointing at me, covering their mouths. My stomach is cramping and I want to fall to the ground, but I run past the teacher, past

Willy and the other kids before finally slowing down so none of them will see I'm about to hurl.

I'm in my bedroom working on the Science Fair project. I've got seven helium balloons of assorted colors, all connected to strings with objects of different weights attached. A red one with a penny tied to it is pressed against the ceiling. Another attached to a textbook is stuck to the ground, reaching. I wonder how many helium balloons it would take to lift me up, fly me away, when my Dad walks in in his camos. He kisses the top of my head, asks what I'm up to, asks if he can help.

"Actually, Dad," I say with a lump in my throat, "I do need your help with something."

He sits on my bed. The princess comforter, which I realize I've outgrown, bunches under him. I stare at his boots.

"Dad, if you do get deployed, if you have to go to Syria, do you think you can find my pen pal for me?"

Of course I don't tell Dad Abdo is my boyfriend because he's old-fashioned, and I don't want him to get the wrong idea. I don't want him to think Abdo is some player, some thug, because he's far from it. He's seen a lot already and is going to be more of a man than any of the boys I go to school with.

"Stephie, honey, I don't think I'll be going to Syria. The President says he doesn't want any American boots on the ground."

"Well why not?" I snap and then change my tone because it's not like I want him to leave. These are tough decisions with no good solutions. "I thought America is supposed to protect the world. I thought we're supposed to save people from the bad guys."

"Yes, usually that's true," Dad says. "But there are too many bad guys in the world for us to save everybody, sweetie. Besides, we've got enough of our own problems here. And our own bad guys too."

Dad tells me Abdo might not even be in Syria anymore. He says millions of people have left the country in the last couple years, thousands every day. They've moved to Lebanon and Jordan and even Iraq. And a lot of people who haven't left Syria have left their homes anyway because they're hungry and scared and don't have jobs. Dad tells me a lot of people have died, and I get mad at him for saying that. There's a horrible crisis there, he says—C-R-I-S-I-S.

The balloons sway in the corner of my room like slow dancers. I know Abdo is still there, still in Damascus. His dad is a member of the Opposition Free Syria Army. His dad is like my dad. No quit. A go-getter. A long time ago Abdo told me if the war kept going on he would have to leave school to fight against the President. Abdo doesn't want to fight. He wants to play soccer. So I know I still have to find a way to save him.

The lights are off and Miss Clark has Google Earth up on the projection screen. Willy's head is down on the desk, buried in his arms. She shows us cities in Syria that have been under attack: Homs, Qusayr, Damascus. She puts a picture up of the President, Bashar al-Assad. He's not what I expected; not an intimidating looking man. He's got a longish neck and a pointy face that makes him look like a ferret. The kind of guy my dad would snap in two.

"Al-Assad ran for President without any competition in two straight elections," Miss Clark says. "Does anyone know why?"

"Because he was so popular no one else thought they had a chance?" someone shouts out.

"Because no one else wanted to be President?"

Miss Clark says we're going to do a mock election and asks for volunteers to run against al-Assad. Willy, of course, jumps up ("Oh-oh-oh!") and shoves Jack Lynch on his way to the front of the room.

"I'm going to kick this guy's butt," Willy says.

"Willy, you may sit down," Miss Clark says before he even gets to her. She explains to him that he and his whole family have been killed because he chose to oppose al-Assad.

"Aw, man," Willy says. "No fair."

She has a few more students come up and they all die too, their families included, and when no one else volunteers she knows we get the point.

The good news, Miss Clark tells us, is despite the war, schools have started to reopen. Hundreds of them. She shows us a picture of kids walking, backpacks on, smiling, past concrete rubble. And for a second I think I haven't outgrown the princess stage after all. Maybe I never will. Maybe when you want something bad enough, fairytales can come true. When you're looking hard enough for answers, they find you. After Social Studies class I hurry over to Miss Clark's desk, rejuvenated. Fruit flies hover over the trash can.

"So Miss Clark? If schools are back in session in Syria, do you think we can start pen palling again this year?"

She looks up at me. She's not grading papers like I expect. She has her phone in front of her, a text message, probably from her boyfriend. She pushes it aside and covers it with her elbow. "I don't think they'll be ready to pen pal for a while, Stephie," she says. "They've got bigger concerns right now, like finding pencils and paper and books."

I can tell she's thinking, *You're just a kid, you don't know how the world works.* She's not saying it, but I can feel it. *One day you'll be all grown up, you'll understand.*

I want to cry. My face is getting warm and tears are building in my eyes so I put my chin down, nod my head, turn and walk back to my desk.

"Besides," Miss Clark says, "mail won't even be delivered to Syria anymore. It's too dangerous. Maybe next year though."

"Uh huh." I keep nodding. Not turning. Just nodding, mumbling. I pull Abdo's birthday card from my backpack, rip it in half, then rip it again, and stuff it back in.

On my way home from school, Willy and his friends spot me as they're cutting across the baseball diamond. "Hey look, a pig escaped from the farm!" he shouts.

Normally I would keep walking, not responding in fear he'll say something else, something meaner, embarrass me even more. But today I don't care. Today I've run out of patience. I drop my bag and charge toward him. Dust rises as I get close.

"C'mon, Willy, let's go. Let's fight right now."

I shove him in the chest. His friends start laughing and then chanting, "Fight, fight, fight."

"C'mon, are you afraid to get beat up by a girl?" I say and shove him a little higher this time, closer to his face.

"Get the fuck off me," Willy says and pushes me away.

That's when I unload. I start swinging at him, eyes half shut, my arms chopping away like the blades of a fan. At some point he puts his hands up to block the blows. I can feel my nails run down his neck, across his cheek, snag his shirt.

"Fuckin' stop," Willy says. He shoots an arm out and pops me in the nose. I'm stunned for a second, a little light-headed. Blood starts trickling down my lip. My mouth tastes like pennies.

"Oh, you hit a girl! Willy hit a girl!" one of his friends says.

"You got your ass kicked by a girl!"

This is going to be big news. I wipe the blood with the back of my arm. It smears across my cheek.

"Crazy bitch," Willy says, covered in scratch marks.

"Asshole," I respond.

I run to our house with its "Lieutenant Colonel Powell and Clan" sign hanging from the front door, its grass cut the exact same length as every other house on base. Soldiers in matching gray T-shirts and shorts jog by along the side of the road, backs sweaty, hollering cadences. "Wimp can't hang, wimp shouldn't have came, 'cause a wimp can be, just like me." This is the safest place in the world.

I burst in, past the family room where Mom is ironing and Paul is watching *SpongeBob*. "Stephie?" Mom says.

I storm into my bedroom and grab the red balloon attached to a coin that can't hold it down. I tape up Abdo's birthday card the best I can, tie it tightly to the string, and run back outside. "What are you doing, Stephie?" Dry blood is crusted on my face, along my arm. I step onto our front lawn and let the balloon go, watch it sail. I know the chance it'll travel across the globe and land in Syria, that Abdo will find it, isn't good. Probably like .000001. I tell myself crazier things have happened. As the balloon rises it gains speed. It scares away a flock of geese and heads straight for a bed of giant white clouds without ever letting up.

SCULPTING SAND

It's just past noon, and I see Casey is finally awake. He's wearing his tie-dye T-shirt, eyeing us from the edge of the beach, sipping on what I assume are two fingers of whiskey from a Styrofoam cup. My wife Sharon is beside me, kneeling under the shade of the umbrella. She's sculpting a sand castle for little Millie who's walking back and forth from the ocean, dumping and re-filling her pail.

A young family from upstate New York has returned from lunch and is making camp next to us. They're renting a beachside cottage for the week too. Their three-year-old stomps through the sand to Millie. She's a walking billboard for Disney in her princess swimsuit, arm floaties, and hat. Sharon and I register these things, these little details, because it's been so many years since we've had to raise a toddler of our own, and I know Sharon is beating herself up for not dressing Millie in a princess suit.

The New Yorker lumbers over to me, a breeze lifting his unbuttoned Cuban shirt and exposing his burnt torso.

I glance at his wife rubbing lotion into her thighs, her beach chair positioned to face the sun. I wish I was thirty again.

"So what do you do up there in The Empire State?" I ask him.

"I'm a therapist."

"How about that. You think I can book a session for my son?" I gesture toward Casey, only half-kidding.

The New Yorker's daughter is pulling sand toys out of Millie's basket, even from her hands. "Don't just take things from her," he tells her. "Ask her nicely." But Millie obliges, has no problem sharing, keeps digging. "What an even-tempered little girl," he says.

I wonder if I should tell him, if it's too much information, but I say it anyway. "She has a heart defect, so she's always been pretty subdued. Tires easily."

He shoots me a sympathetic glance, doesn't say much. Most people don't know how to respond, even shrinks I guess.

"The doctors were ready to operate when she was born," I say, "but she came out healthy. A miracle, really. The problem is her body is getting too big now for her heart."

He nods, tells me he's sorry, and then stares across the horizon. I spare him the specifics. That she has L-Transposition of the great arteries, a large VSD, pulmonary stenosis, and constrictions in her heart's blood vessel.

"How 'bout a beer?" I ask him. "Or a bourbon?" He declines.

It's not that I care, because I could give two shits, but I'm curious what he's thinking. I'm often curious what people are thinking when they see Sharon and me with Millie. Especially when they find out she has a heart problem. I look at the shrink, eyes hidden behind his aviator shades, and I wonder if he's blaming us. If he's surmising we're two irresponsible old fuckers who decided to have a kid at our age. It doesn't take a shrink, though, to understand you never know what the story is behind closed doors.

Casey and I are walking along the shore, under a cloudless sky and an unyielding sun. I'm pulling Millie along in her red wagon. My sandals sink into the powdery sand with each step.

"So tell me about Utah?" I say.

"I'd rather not talk about it right now."

"I paid thirty thousand dollars to send you there. I saved you from getting locked up for half a year. Don't you think I deserve to know how it went?"

"I said I don't want to talk about it." Casey's hair falls over his brow and he flicks his head, this annoying head flick he and all his friends do.

There are happy couples walking by us, families, sunbathers and joggers all around too, so I don't press him any further. "Okay, all right."

Casey has spent the last two months in a wilderness camp after a string of run-ins with the Menasha Police. Possession of marijuana with the intent to sell (he swore he was just smoking with Hannah, his on-again, off-again girlfriend, and the little extra bag they had in the car was only for them), possession of stolen property (cash taken from area vending machines by a friend who owed him for reasons we could assume), and possession of marijuana while on probation. The police have come to know Casey well, have had it out for him I think. It's a small town we live in, only about 17,000 people. One of the Fox Cities in eastern Wisconsin running along the banks of the Fox River. The police don't have a whole lot to do there and, in fairness, neither do the kids.

"Have you heard from Hannah?" I ask him.

"Yeah, she says she has a lawyer. Supposedly, she's got a job now, doing better. She's going to try to get custody."

Seagulls circle overhead, eyeing picnic spreads. Millie sings Disney songs to herself from the wagon. We start heading up toward the low-rise condos dotting the beach, painted in calming pastels. Salmon, cream, peach.

"Let's just get through Millie's surgery next month," I say. "We've always said you and Hannah are her rightful mom and dad, so that would be the goal." This is the message I've been repeating to myself for three years.

My mother is sitting in a beach chair, protected by the shade of the cottage, and sipping on a Manhattan. I convinced her to join us on this trip. Thought it'd be good for her. For Casey too. Having his granny with him, reminding him who he is deep down under the layers of regret and failed dreams.

"Hi, Mom." She doesn't hear me. Has no idea what we've been through the last couple years or where Casey has been for the past two months. As far as she knows, he's a typical twenty-year-old, slogging through college courses and hanging out with pals. She brags about him to her friends because people only see what they want to.

"Why don't we go in for lunch?" I tell Casey.

"I'll be there in a minute."

He stays outside to have a cigarette while I pull Millie out of the wagon and carry her into the cottage.

Millie is napping. Casey is too. Sharon and I sit in the kitchen, talking quietly over the whir of the tropical ceiling fan. The lime green walls are covered in ceramic starfish and crabs and a wooden sign with a painting of a margarita glass that reads, "What Happens at the Beach, Stays at the Beach."

"He doesn't want to accept any responsibility for her," Sharon says. "He acts like she's not even his."

"Let's give them some time together. Maybe this week will do them good."

"Utah hasn't changed him at all. And you've been bending over backward for him."

She says it like it's a bad thing, me trying to keep our kid from sinking, from getting swallowed up by the Earth. She's already given me a hard time about hiring him as a receptionist at my law office and setting up an apprenticeship with a Fox Cities real estate big shot. I'm paying Casey's salary with the guy, though Casey's not aware of that. I know there's a fine line between helping and enabling. I understand that, but every father wants to see his son become a man.

I tell Sharon about Hannah. About her wanting custody. Her eyes get wide, she puts her hand over her mouth, stands up to give her something to do other than cry. Because of her heart and Hannah's drug use and emotional problems, we've had custody of Millie since the day she was born. At first, it was just to protect her, give her a chance at life. We said if the kids ever got their shit together we'd give Millie back to them, her rightful parents. It's hard not to feel like she's ours now, though, with everything we've sacrificed, how much our life has changed. For the better in a lot of ways. Sharon had to give up her career as a stone sculptor to take care of Millie. She misses it every day but if it's between sculpting and Millie, there's no competition. After three years, we feel like she deserves nothing less than what we've been giving her.

"She can't even take care of herself, and she thinks she can take care of a child?" Sharon says to no one in particular.

"He says she's getting her life together."

"She still smokes around Millie. Even with her heart problems."

These are all things I know well, but I nod anyway. I get up to pour myself a bourbon.

"What did we do wrong?" Sharon asks.

"Maybe we were too hard on him growing up."

"Or maybe we were too easy."

Sharon and I smoked plenty of pot when we were Casey's age. We named him after the Grateful Dead song that was playing when we met, for God's sake, but we ended up being productive adults, law abiding citizens. I've told Casey, but should I have? It was more cautionary than anything, like, *Look, we were teenagers once too, and we know you're going to drink and we know you're going to smoke a little weed, but be careful. Be smart. This isn't your father's weed. It's a hell of a lot more potent these days, more addictive.* Who knows, maybe it kept him from moving on to harder stuff. Parenting is full of second-guessing. Even the New Yorker will see that someday.

"We've always known this was a possibility," I tell Sharon. "We've always said they're the rightful parents. We just need to get through the surgery."

In the monitor, we see Millie moving in her bed. Sharon goes in, brushes her hair from her face and kisses her forehead. I check on Casey in the next room and he's lying face up, not moving, like a corpse. The bed sheets smell like cigarette smoke. I put my hand to his chest to see if I can feel it rise and fall, to make sure he's alive. He lets out a deep breath that startles me. I cover him with the sheet and tiptoe back out.

The sun is beginning to set, and fishermen and seagulls have taken over the beach. We're on a dolphin cruise of the upper Boca Ciega Bay, sailing past mangrove islands and million-dollar homes. Beer and hotdogs are being served from a cooler out of the front of the catamaran. We're fifteen minutes in and have already seen two bottlenose dolphins leap from the water. Millie's joy—seeing dolphins for the first time and jumping up, no less—is worth the fourteen hundred miles we've traveled.

The tour guide announces over the mic that a dolphin is riding the bow wave of the boat, and passengers stand up, pull out their cameras, start taking video. Casey picks Millie up and takes her to see. They're hanging over the edge of the boat.

"Be careful," Sharon says to him. "It's bumpy."

"Let 'em be," I say.

Millie is squealing in delight, the wind blowing her hair back. It pushes her hat right off her head. Sharon and

I look at each other and are both thinking the same thing. Casey is on his second beer and who knows how much booze he had this morning, how much is still in his system. By instinct, my eyes locate the hook ladder and life rings.

"She's fine," I tell Sharon and force a smile.

Casey is laughing too, and I see a glimpse of the old version of him, before the Phish tours and tie-dye T-shirts, before the long hair and the head flicking. A thought pops into my mind, this horrible thought, that the birth of Millie ruined his life. Maybe he would have gone down a normal path if he hadn't had to deal with becoming a father at seventeen, the father of a sick kid at that. Was he getting high to escape, to forget about the fact his life was irreversibly changed?

Casey looks at us, still smiling, and shakes his head like he can see the dread in our eyes, the distrust, trying to tell us, *You two are over the top, stop worrying so much, I'm going to be okay this time.*

"Dolphin, dolphin!" Millie screams, alternating between turning away scared and leaning back over the edge to get another look.

The next morning, I sit on the balcony and have my morning coffee. The wind chimes jingle. A brown anole lizard scales the wall. It's another day of hoping the rising ocean sun will thaw our hearts before the Wisconsin snow has even had a chance.

By nine, the kids are still asleep. My mom is in the family room watching a game show on TV. Sharon and I decide to go to the local Publix to stock up.

"Be back soon, Mom," I say.

When we return, my mom is still in front of the TV, but Millie and Casey are nowhere to be found. Their empty cereal bowls are in the sink, their flip-flops gone.

"Hey mom, where are the kids?" Sharon asks.

"They were just here. Aren't they here?" She's got a mimosa in front of her, and I wonder if she's smashed already.

It's not even noon, so Casey being awake, let alone out of the house, is suspicious. And Millie is a creature of habit. She likes her thirty minutes of Disney cartoons on the iPad before starting the day. Sharon calls Casey's phone, but it goes straight to his voicemail.

"They probably went down to the beach," I say.

The New Yorkers are there. The man is setting up their umbrella, the woman basting their daughter in sunscreen. The sand sculptures Sharon built for Millie the day before have melted back into the ground and are nothing more than mounds. I don't see Casey or Millie anywhere.

"Good morning," they say.

"Good morning. Have you seen our brood, by chance?" I ask.

"No, haven't seen them," the man says. "Not down here."

A little panic starts to set in. I can see it in Sharon's face too. Fear something terrible has happened. Millie's been kidnapped by Casey, Hannah is in on it too. We've let our guard down too much, I've let my guard down, and have fallen victim to an intricate plan. We'll never see Millie's sweet face again. It's a fear even worse than that of her impending surgery, if that's possible, of her not making it through.

I'm too embarrassed to explain the situation to the New Yorkers, to the shrink. What would I even say? *We can't find our daughter who's really our son's daughter but who's kind of like our own daughter because our son is a druggie and, yeah, by the way, we really fucked up raising him. What do you make of that, doc? What diagnosis do you have for this family dynamic?* I turn and almost trip over the girl's sand toys.

We jump into the minivan, crunch over the seashells for a driveway, and start scouring the town. Sharon isn't talking, just searching out the window, left then right. Not at the playground, not climbing the dolphin statue at the Welcome Center, not feeding the turtles at the nature preserve. We cross the causeway and head out of the tourist territory, get lost among the locals. He wouldn't have gone to score some weed with her, would he have? Past tattoo parlors. Past bait & tackle, ammo and pawn shops.

"I'm sure it's fine," I say, but Sharon doesn't respond. I know, in her head, she's blaming me—*If something bad happened, I swear*, she's thinking. Blaming me for giving Casey a second chance when tough love should have been the only option. And I think I see what Sharon has been seeing for a while: if we're forced to choose between Casey and Millie at this point, Millie wins.

Then, as we head back over the causeway, down Gulf Boulevard toward the cottage, there they are. Casey and Millie, strolling down the sidewalk, holding hands. Each with an ice-cream cone in the other hand. Millie with chocolate, her favorite, melting down her arm. Casey with what I'm guessing is Rocky Road, his usual pick.

Sharon and I look at each other, not with a smirk, not like we've caught ourselves being foolish, because, really, who would feel any differently in our position? We step out of the car and approach them.

Millie has chocolate circling her mouth. We can scold Casey for not sending us a text message letting us know where they went or for giving her ice-cream before lunch, but we don't. We wouldn't dare.

"Well hey," Sharon says. "Did you two have fun?" Millie runs into her arms.

I've come to accept that if we're going to make it through this ordeal, it's going to have to be one day at a time. That's what they preach in recovery. And that's what Sharon and I have been telling each other since we found out about Millie's complicated heart. Maybe someday Casey and I will get matching tattoos, father and son, and that's what they'll say. In painful black ink: *One day at a time*.

KINDA SORTA AMERICAN DREAM

I'm in the supper line behind fifty white-bearded fat asses ready to stack my plate high with fried chicken, buttered egg noodles, and creamy cabbage salad. Might as well get something out of this. "Welcome Class of 2012" is spelled out above the dinner choices on the menu board. When we graduate—those of us who do—we'll be the seventy-fifth group to stake that claim. I dropped out of community college after one year and always preferred Halloween over Christmas, so the fact that I'm here, at the Harvard of Santa schools so they say, makes it plain just how twisted life is.

I find a seat at an empty table, bread buns rolling off my plate like snowballs.

"Sit over here, pal," one of the Santas calls out to me.

"Saved this spot for you."

"Come on, join us!"

It's amazing how exaggerated friendliness is here.

"Thanks, fellas," I say.

For a lot of these guys, this isn't their first rodeo. Unlike me, most are retired and have been playing Santa for years to make a little extra income. I'm sandwiched between an ex-land surveyor and an aerospace engineer. An agricultural salesman is slurping down a casserole right in my face. Some of these guys have been here before and are signed on for a tune-up, you know, to work on the ho-ho-ho or pick up new tips on beard grooming. One Santa—Gill—is already getting on my last nerve. He's Southern-California-tan, bragging to us about how he doesn't need the money, how he volunteers his time at hospitals and village tree lightings. I want to reach across the table and smack him upside the head with a drumstick.

From the windows, we can see flakes beginning to fall. Gill, of course, breaks out into song—"Let it Snow"—and pretty soon the whole cafeteria is rockin'. I feel like quite the imposter because, I'm embarrassed to admit, I don't even remember the words. I'm no Santa. At six four, a hundred ninety pounds wet, I look more like Frankenstein than anything. I scan the room, move my lips, bounce my head anyway. I do my best to stumble through it without letting on how lost I am.

"I don't feel comfortable here," I tell Barb.

We're in our dorm room. She doesn't respond or even look up, just keeps unpacking her suitcase and putting clothes in drawers. Her not saying anything says a lot.

Like, "Well, you better suck it up, Wayne, unless you got a better idea because as of now we've run out of options."

"Mom paid," she finally says, "and we're already here."

My mother-in-law, The Meddler, saw a segment about this place on *20/20*. Since I've been out of work a while, she forked out the cash for this mini-camp and sent us as an "early Christmas gift." In three days I'm supposed to miraculously be transformed into Santa and Barb into Mrs. Claus. The Meddler said it would give us the chance to find seasonal work, and when she said it I could tell she thought of herself as quite the do-gooder, which royally pissed me off. But Barb decided it might be a good idea for us to give this a try, and I'm in no position to argue with her.

"I'm going to call and see how the boys are doing," Barb says, her hair dyed white and pulled up into a bun, which is still wigging me out.

Before the plant shut down almost a year ago, we paid our mortgage on time for a nice ranch outside Detroit, Barb stayed home with the boys—now fourteen, eleven, and six—and I made a modest living. We'd take summer camping trips to Muskegon or Ossineke, had even been to Canada once. We were kinda sorta living the American Dream. The boys haven't wanted much to do with me in my recent mood state, and now they're crashing with their grandpa and The Meddler who I'm sure are doing their best to convince them they're better caretakers than us.

"Do you want to say goodnight to Dad?" Barb says. "Boys? Oh hey, Mom. Where'd they go?" She glances at me and shrugs.

"Guess not," I mumble.

The room smells like peppermint. Coupled with the Christmas decorations it's smothered in—a candy cane bedspread, creepy talking Santa doll, wooden nutcrackers—I feel nauseous, like I've eaten too much candy. Even though I know it's not for the best, I wish I was back in the comforts of my own home. I wish I was alone in my den, where I feel safe at least, searching for jobs that don't exist or that I'm not qualified for, obsessively checking my family's online bank account, watching our savings slowly disappear.

It's the ass crack of dawn, the Dean of the school is at the podium in the front of the great hall (interestingly, the only guy in here with a clean shave), and I'm sipping on burnt coffee out of a Styrofoam cup. I can't stop scratching my neck because my newly dyed beard, only three-week's growth at this point, is itching to no end. I flip through the schedule: non-stop sessions on marketing and promotion, fitness training, and posing techniques to name a few. On the last page I read "Final Test (Hint: In Front of TV Cameras)," and my stomach churns.

"Kids expect perfection," the Dean says. "That means you need to have fresh-smelling breath, know all the reindeer names, act like you've lived in the North Pole your whole life. And it helps to have real reindeer doo doo on the soles of your shoes."

The Santas laugh in unison—a hearty laughter that rumbles from deep within their bowels. The white Santas, the Latino Santas, the one black Santa even. I'm having a hard time understanding what's so funny, especially at the crack of dawn's ass.

"Give it your all on every effort," the Dean continues, "because each kid will remember you forever. To be a great Santa, you have to want to be him, embody his spirit, be willing to stay in character through highs and lows. I'm a firm believer you don't choose to be Santa, you're chosen to be."

I roll my eyes and search the crowd for someone sharing my skepticism—a raised eyebrow, folded arms— but the rest of these suckers are all nodding their heads in agreement, hands on bellies.

"Enough from me," the Dean says. "Let's go around and have each of you share your name and your wildest Christmas story."

As if a switch is turned on, my heart begins hammering away at my chest cavity, and I know where this is going so I bail. I mutter something to the Santa next to me about having to hit the head, though I really don't care if he hears. Barb is running late to her Mrs. Claus meeting and is still in our room, slipping into her plaid worsted cloak.

She looks like Mrs. Doubtfire, and that actually calms me a bit.

"I can't do this," I say. "I'm freaking out. They're having us get up and talk about ourselves and we're supposed to be all cool and jolly."

"Why don't you take one of your Xanax, Wayne? Did you take your Xanax?"

"I hate having to rely on that stuff." I shake one out from the pill container anyway and fire it down my throat.

"You'll be fine," Barb says as she squeezes her hooves into black pointed shoes with fancy gold buckles we're supposed to presume were fashioned by elves. She stopped comforting me during these episodes months ago, and I'm not sure if she's just fed up or if it's tough love.

"All right, I guess I'll deal with it myself then," I say.

"Wayne, c'mon."

Six months back, I started waking up in the middle of the night scared I was about to die. The weirdest things are setting me off now on a regular basis. High school fears like speaking in public, talking to attractive ladies, calling about job openings.

I step closer to the door. I can still hear Santas bellowing into the microphone: "Next thing I know my leg starts feeling wet and, sure enough, the kid's taking a leak on me!"

For some reason, I think of the boys, especially my fourteen-year-old, and I'm glad they're not here to see me pacing the room, shrinking behind the door. The schedule, rolled up in my fist, is tight enough to make a straw. I peer down at letters following the paper's curve, namely the letters "T" and "V." The boys would love to see their old man on the tube, wouldn't they? A younger version of me would have been the first to jump in front of television cameras and act a fool. I was the goof in the high school cafeteria doing magic tricks for crowds, making coins disappear in my hand, but now look at me. I crumple up the schedule into a furious little ball and dunk it into the snowman-shaped garbage bin.

That afternoon, we're at a toy store in a local mall doing field research on the latest crazes: Furby, Elmo Live, something called a Lalaloopsy Silly Hair Star doll. Gill is examining a box holding a One Direction action figure. I believe it's Harry Styles, and I only know this because Barb says our fourteen-year-old is growing his hair out to look like him. He cares more about his Harry Styles hair, in fact, than about his grades from what she tells me.

I see Gill nudge Barb who's standing beside him. "One Direction?" he says. "Who are these guys? What happened to The Monkees and The Beatles, right? Now those were bands." He cackles like it's the funniest thing he's said—ever—and Barb obliges him with a laugh herself.

I'm a few feet away, staring at a Ninjago Epic Battle Lego set, clawing at my beard, pretending not to pay any mind.

"Do you have any kids?" Gill asks her, this guy with his orange skin and white teeth, this George Hamilton in a Santa suit.

"Three," Barb says. "All boys."

"Three boys? You've got to be a saint, right? I'm in the presence of sainthood, and I don't mean Saint Nick. No offense to you, buddy," he says, turning to me. Cackle, cackle. "How old are they?"

"The oldest is fourteen…"

"There's no way you have a fourteen-year-old. Get out! Even if you are supposed to be Mrs. Claus."

"I do, believe it or not. The next one is eleven and the youngest is—"

"Six," I interrupt. "The little guy's six."

Gill's eyes get wide as truck tires. He nods his head, giggles out of place, and goes back to fumbling with the Harry box. Barb pulls a doll from the shelf and clears her throat. She inadvertently presses its belly, and the doll shouts, "I made a stinky!" I maneuver one of the little ninja Lego soldiers and poke his sword into the monstrous snake with its red eyes and silver fangs. Gill puts Harry away and moseys out of the aisle, beginning a carol under his breath.

The next morning, the Santas are assembled in the great hall. The toy train is chugging its way around trays of pineapple and Danishes. I'm downing my black coffee and eavesdropping on conversations. "How'd you get your beard to smell like a candy cane?" one Santa says to another. "Peppermint oil," the other one says. "That's my little secret." I roll my eyes. A three-hundred pound candy cane all right.

The Dean gets up to the podium and announces what's on tap for the day: dance lessons and sessions on liability insurance and make-up artistry. A child psychologist will be lecturing us too.

"Before I send you off to your first session, let's talk about tomorrow's final project," the Dean says. My chest tightens. "You've all been paired up and will take turns playing Santa at various locations across the area—daycare centers, old age homes, churches. Local newspaper and TV crews will be floating around to catch you in action."

That familiar feeling joins me as the Santas are bumping past to find out their assignments. I'm short of breath and my mouth tastes like I'm sucking on batteries for mints. I'm caught in the stream of Santas, following the scent of peppermint and body odor, but inside I want to run. Inside, I'm a caveman with a saber-tooth on his trail.

I don't even have the chance to open the card with my name on it before Gill's warm breath is heating my neck. "You're the only Wayne P. I take it, right?"

"Uh, yeah, I think so."

He extends his hand and grasps my sweaty palm. "Looks like it's you and me then, buddy. Our gig's at the Midland Mall. That's gotta be the primo assignment, right? Am I right?"

I stare at the raspberry jelly squeezing out of Gill's Danish and onto his pearly whites. A Santa nudges my shoulder from behind, and a speckle of coffee lands on my shirt. "Whoa, you okay, buddy?" Gill says. "You don't look too good. Bleach in your beard getting to you?"

The music begins to blare over the loudspeakers, signaling us to move on to our first session of the day, and I'm off to the Rudolph Room to learn how to do the Christmas Waltz. Between Bing Crosby's "Silver Bells" and Gill's cackling there's no time to think, and that's probably exactly what I need.

Barb and I are lying in bed watching the news. A blizzard is blowing in, they say. Over a foot of snow is expected to drop by tomorrow afternoon. Outside our window, things seem calm for now. A lamppost lights the mounds of snow, the lot of them glazed with a thin veil of ice, that have set up camp right there for the winter.

"Maybe they'll cancel this stupid final project," I say.

Barb doesn't look at me, only tucks her white locks behind her ears, pushes up her glasses with her trigger finger. "One more day, Wayne. And just think, once you have a diploma from here, you'll be like a Super Santa. You'll be able to work wherever you want I bet."

"Super Santa. Fantastic, what I've always aspired to be. I can be like the jerkoff they've paired me up with."

"Oh c'mon, Gill seems like a nice guy."

"He's not. But the good thing is, I'm sure his pompous ass will have no problem doing the whole gig on his own and I can sit back, blow smoke up his rear, and finish up so we can go home already."

"You should hang out with Gill, regain your confidence. It doesn't seem like anything bothers him. That's the way you used to be before all this."

This has an assortment of connotations and hangs in the air like God-awful breath. For ten years running I was racking up World's Best Dad T-shirts and mugs each Christmas. Now whose fault is it I can't keep up the act? Whose fault is it I'm reduced to vying for the title of Super Santa?

"So, what," I say, "do you want to fuck the guy?" Barb's head whips around, and she glares at me, eyes crazy, mouth like a giant sinkhole. "I'm sorry, that was dumb."

She jumps out of the bed. "What's wrong with you? Have you completely lost your mind?"

She storms into the bathroom, slams the door, and locks it. That doesn't stop her from yelling at me though, and I'm a little embarrassed thinking if anyone hears us it may dampen the Christmas cheer. "Now that your family needs you to step up," Barb says, "all you want to do is hide in your den like a damn groundhog waiting for the spring!"

"I'm sorry."

"I mean, what kind of man have you become?"

She keeps going like that for a while. Comments of that nature that slowly taper off. When she comes out an hour later, even after I say "Sorry" for the umpteenth time, she doesn't make eye-contact or respond. She gets into bed and we lay with our backs to each other. I can't sleep, and she periodically kicks the sheets and readjusts her pillow so I don't suppose she's sleeping much either. I gaze out the window wondering how I let *this* go so far. Then snowflakes start to fall at some dreadful hour, and I assume the blizzard has burst through the gates.

I'm the first Santa in the great hall. It's as quiet as this place has been, and even the Christmas lights haven't been turned on yet. The Dean is getting the coffee brewed. I reach for a gingerbread scone from the breakfast table. "Is it okay if I grab one of these?"

"Oh yeah, sure. Early bird gets the worm, right?"

I stare out at the snow falling down sideways, the wind combing the evergreens back like a big brush. The Dean seems unfazed, goes back to the kitchen and brings out a fruit platter, like it's just another day in the North Pole. I catch a glimpse of his Mrs. reaching for plates from a cabinet.

"So what line of work are you in back home," the Dean says, "you know, when you're not donning the Santa costume?"

"I worked at a plant that manufactured parts for the auto companies. Drive line parts mostly. Front and rear axles, propeller shafts. I was on the assembly line for seventeen years, but the plant closed down for good about a year ago. Been out of work since."

"Nothing else out there, huh?"

"Nothing else I know how to do."

"Well you came to the right place."

"I suppose," I say.

"You got kids, Santa?"

"Three."

"Well, if there's any good in this it's that you'll be able to relate as well as anyone when you have that sad little child on your lap asking you to get his daddy a job or help them keep their house."

A few groggy Santas, half-asleep, drag themselves into the hall. They nod their heads and mumble "Good morning" before lining up for coffee.

"Where you headed this afternoon?" the Dean asks me.

"Midland Mall. With good ol' Gill."

"Oh boy, guess you didn't hear. Gill went out skiing at Apple Mountain last night. Broke his leg. You won't be seeing him unless you plan on visiting the MidMichigan Medical Center."

"So what the hell does that mean for me?"

"I guess it means you're on your own, Santa. Think you can handle a mall full of overexcited kids?"

Fortunately, the mall is pretty much a straight shot down 10 because I'm on my own and I can't see out of the windshield even with the wipers going full force. Barb is with the other ladies probably learning how to bake cookies. Even if she wasn't she wouldn't be with me. She hasn't talked to me since last night and I'm sure she doesn't think I'd muster the balls to do this mall thing which may very well be the reason I'm going.

With the snow, I'm expecting a light crowd, but of course it comes to a stop as soon as I get out of the truck. Because that's the twisted nature of this life. A plow is crashing through the lot, clearing the way for all the minivans and little tykes I imagine are eagerly throwing on their coats and boots in foyers across town. Inside, the mall is set for my arrival. In the center of the courtyard, behind kiosks selling chair massages and pillow pets, there's a towering tree with red and green ornaments.

Beside it, there's a gold throne, my throne, surrounded by poinsettias and phony gift boxes. Carols are piping through the loudspeakers: "You better watch out, you better not cry…" It reminds me of a time not that long ago but that seems long ago when I was the one on the other side of the red velvet rope with my three boys. To be honest, I don't even know if my six-year-old still believes in Santa.

I meet up with the general manager, a chubby fella with a five o'clock shadow who looks like he could be a mall Santa too if he wasn't running this joint. He walks me into a back room, makes me sign some papers, and invites me to go ahead and get suited up. He wishes me a Merry Christmas in the same way a church-goer would say "Bless you, Father" to a priest, and then walks out.

I'm alone for the first time in full costume—suit, boots, hat, and gold-rimmed glasses. I examine myself in a smudged face mirror stuck to a file cabinet and realize it's been a while since I've done so. I don't look anything like me, but it is me. I don't think I look much like Santa either, but as long as the kids buy what I'm selling, as long as one of them doesn't sniff me out, this can end up all right. I grab a Snickers from the vending machine and wolf it down for a little boost.

As I'm heading to my throne, I start feeling weak, hyperventilating. I try to remember everything I've absorbed over the last three days despite putting so much effort into not paying attention to any of it. "Keep your hands in plain view, keep your hands in plain view, keep your hands in plain view," I'm muttering under my breath. I give my mustache a little curl because it apparently gives more of a fantasy look, adds to the magic that is Santa. The line is building, I see, into a mass of moms and strollers, winter coats and runny noses. The mall photographer is setting up, and I spot a TV crew lurking by the RadioShack. I can't feel my beard itch. I'm not sure if that's a good thing.

My phone begins vibrating in my pocket. I'm worried if someone sees me answering it I can get in trouble because maybe Santa isn't supposed to have a phone. But then again they're presumably making all these toys in the North Pole, right, so why wouldn't they have phones too in this day and age? Plus, it might be an emergency so I pull it out. It's Barb.

"What's up?" I say. "I'm about to go on," thinking she's calling to give me some last minute moral support, declare how much she believes in me.

"I just had a call from my mom," she says. "Are you sitting?"

"Yes I'm sitting. I'm sitting in my Santa throne."

"Your son decided to sneak out of the house last night. My parents found out when the police brought him home around midnight after they caught him drinking beer with two of his friends in an alley."

"You're telling me this now?"

My immediate reaction is to race out of here because I have a legitimate excuse. I'll do the three hour drive home in two, grab my boy and shake him. My boy who I've barely spoken to the past six months, my boy who's growing his hair out to resemble a British pop star. As much as I'd like to ask him what he was thinking—*why?*—I know he won't have a good answer, and I already kinda sorta know why anyway. Besides, I have an army of toddlers that will hunt me down and trample me into the snow if I run for it at this point.

"I'm sorry I'm laying this on," Barb says. "I just had to tell you."

"I don't know what to say."

"Mom and Dad have been keeping an eye on him all day. We'll deal with this tonight. No point in leaving now anyway because we'll just get stuck on the highway with this snow."

"Ready Santa?" the GM calls.

No, no I'm not. But "ho, ho" is what comes out of my mouth.

"Good luck," Barb says. "I'm proud of you, Wayne."

The first kid is being dragged toward me by his mom, and I don't have time to cry or yell or scrutinize my parenting. The kid is clinging to his mom as they near, terrified, like if he comes to me he'll be swallowed up into the abyss that is my fluffy red suit. The mom tries to drop him in my lap, but his arms are locked around her neck.

"It's okay, little pal, you can come here," I say.

"Oh he did this last year too," the mom says, swiping her dangling brown hair from her eyes.

Then why the hell did you bring him back? I'm thinking.

"Come on, sweetie," the mom pleads, "Santa just wants to know what you want for Christmas."

The kid is finally in my lap, but writhing, arching his back, one arm grasping his mom's top.

In a panic, I start thinking *WWGD—What Would Gill Do?* "Do you want to hear all about my reindeers?" I say. "Donner, Blitzer." But he doesn't stop thrashing.

So I dig into my pocket and pull out a quarter. "Hey, hey, watch, little buddy. Watch what Santa can do."

He quiets a bit, his chest still heaving though, snot running down his lip. He sneezes on me. I show him the coin between my thumb and index finger. "Should we make it disappear?" I ask, and he nods. I swipe my right hand over the coin as if I'm grabbing it and then squeeze the hand shut. "Go ahead and blow on it," I say.

He looks to his mom for reassurance. "Blow on it, sweetie," she says, and so he does. Then I slowly fan my fingers open for the big reveal and, lo and behold, the coin has vanished as far as the little guy can tell. His eyes widen. It's the same expression my boys used to have when I would do the same trick for them. They'd gawk at me in amazement as if I was other-worldly, invincible, like they couldn't believe I was their dad. I was pretty sure they'd never doubt me for a second.

By the time I make the coin reappear behind the kid's ear, he's not crying anymore. In fact, he's twiddling with my mustache. His mom backs away a few steps, and the photographer snaps a picture I have to believe is a good one.

"Okay, so now let's get down to business, little man," I say. "What is it you want Santa to get you for Christmas?"

IT TAKES A VILLAGE

Andrew's new boss noticed him staring at her calf tattoo while she searched her file cabinet for school policies on hazing, drug use, and food allergies. The tattoo was a jumble of letters in a language he didn't speak.

"You like that?" Sherri said. "It means 'I have hope' in Zulu."

Her whole office was an extension of her spider-veined calf, actually, a gallery of inspirational phrases. Andrew considered it a good omen. Above her desk, a framed picture of an empty canoe against the shore read, "If the wind will not serve, take to the oars." A plaque hanging from her door declared, "Don't be afraid to stand for what you believe in, even if it means standing alone."

"Here's some light reading for you," Sherri said, handing him copies of documents with wrinkled corners and lipstick smudges. She laughed longer and harder than she should have.

The social worker in Andrew surfaced, and he began his analysis: bulging eyes, skin hanging off her limbs, the fat in her body poking out unevenly like soup cans in a grocery bag. Some teachers came back from summer break with new hairdos. He surmised gastric bypass had been part of Sherri's big summer plans. Her exaggerated positivity likely disguised deep-rooted insecurity. He wanted to comfort her.

"Get here early, leave late. Be visible. Trust me, people will warm to you," she said.

Andrew took notes. "Let me know if you have any questions, okay kiddo? I know you're on a one-year contract and all, but if you do well and the powers that be like you, if you save some of our troubled youth that'll be walking through those doors in about thirty minutes, there's no reason you can't stay with us permanently, all right?"

"I'm grateful to be here. I'll do my best."

A teacher popped her head into Sherri's office for the next appointment. "Now go get 'em."

Andrew held the stack of papers to his chest, pamphlets on sexting and cyberbullying falling from his grasp, as he got up from the chair. On his way out, he rubbed the belly of her porcelain Buddha for luck.

Cole woke up to his mom smoking at the edge of his bed, ash peppering the carpet. "Get your ass up," she said. "We're not doing this. Get up—now."

He was in the middle of a dream where he was hidden in bushes, staring through a bathroom window at a freckle-skinned woman lathering in a steamy shower. He was not happy to be awakened from it. And he was not happy to have his mom sitting on his bed while he sported wood. "Get outta here," he said and kicked her in the ribs.

"I'm going to call your dad to come and beat the crap out of you if you kick me again."

He kicked her again, not only because he wanted to, but because his dad hadn't been around in eight months despite the dozens of times she'd threatened to have him storm over.

"When I come back, you better be up," she said. "I'm not having you miss the first day of school so they can call and harass me about it."

"Close the fuckin' door when you leave my room!"

Cole's bleary eyes opened to posters of Drake and Megan Fox hanging above old gold-plated Little League trophies and conch shells hiding the ocean's roar. His mom's big ass had left its imprint in the bed's foam. He reached for his phone under the pillow. He checked Facebook, Twitter, texts: "Can I like not go back to school?" "Is it Friday yet?" "Waking up before ten should be illegal #schoolsucks #summerforeva."

He slowly got up because he knew the deal. His mom had bought him new clothes, hats, and diamond studs, so he promised to actually try in school this year. It wasn't beyond her to throw them all out if he didn't at least pretend to cooperate. But the promise had come in July, when August 20 was in the distant future, and now it was August 20 already. He tweeted: "Wtf." Back to his school full of Taylor Swift-loving biatches. He mulled over arguments for why there was no point in going on the first day: 1) you didn't do shit on the first day, 2) everyone he wanted to see he saw every day anyway, 3) he didn't want to run into his ex with her new boyfriend because he'd end up smashing the kid's teeth in, get suspended, blah blah blah.

"You remember our deal!" his mom hollered up the stairs. A Dr. Phil rerun blared from the kitchen.

By eight, the school bell was ringing, and Cole was still sculpting his fauxhawk because if it didn't look right there was no point in showing his face, even though he was going to wear a hat over it anyway. The yellow Hummer was idling in the driveway, Cole's mom honking the horn with one hand, the other holding a lit Virginia Slim out the window. He put on his new True Religion tee and jeans and stepped into the car at 8:11.

"This is your last chance," she said. "You hear me? If you screw this year up, you're done. You're off to military school."

He put his Beats on, and she yanked them off. "Are you listening to me, you little shit?"

"No, I'm listening to Lil Wayne."

"That's it, I'm calling your dad today." She took a deep drag. "Consider this strike one."

She dropped him off under the clock tower beside the palm tree at 8:17. He went inside the building and texted his boys: "YOLO." When he saw the Hummer turn the corner, he walked back out and met up with them. By 8:22, they were high behind the Arby's.

Andrew spent the morning in his cramped office with no windows putting up pictures, organizing his bookshelf, and devising an action plan. Now he was in the faculty cafeteria having lunch with the Special Educators. There was no better way to get the lay of the land than mixing it up with the locals. Tomorrow he would sit with the Social Science folks, Wednesday with Fine Arts, and so on.

One of the teachers, Big Brad (self-proclaimed), had taken to him. He had sweat above his lip. He pointed to what was left of the coffee and scones, compliments of the administration, spread out across a folding table. "Don't expect to get anything free from those fuckers again this year," Big Brad said. He got up to wrap several of the blueberry-almond variety in napkins before stuffing them in short pockets veiled by his Hawaiian shirt.

The others at the table were talking about summer break, how it had gone too quickly, how the last thing they wanted was to be back at school, at this school. They complained about the heat, the giant mosquitos, the rain—the constant rain—and joked about how wrong it was to be so pissed off already when it was only the first day. Andrew, at the end of the table, nodded and smiled while he munched on a Cuban sandwich, trying to find an in, some common ground.

"Are you new here?" an older woman in a loose necktie, hair gelled back, finally asked him. Andrew appreciated her hospitality.

"Yes, yeah, actually, new to Florida as well. My wife and I just moved here from Chicago a couple months ago. We thought a change of scenery would be good for us."

"Wow, Chi-cah-go," the woman said, her voice adopting a nasal quality presumably to mimic the accent Andrew never knew he had. The Special Educators laughed.

"So you came all the way from Chi-cah-go to work at this place?" someone else chimed in, and there were more laughs. Andrew could feel red blotches colonizing his neck. He buried his face in his Cuban.

"The morale here's a bit low," Big Brad said.

He filled Andrew in on the new administration, a crackerjack principal the school recruited from the East Coast two years back who was tanner than any Floridian (rumor was he had a tanning bed in his office) and the cronies he'd slowly brought on board. The principal was a short guy who had been given the unofficial nickname, "Little Napoleon." Big Brad told Andrew about the new teacher contract that had taken a year for both sides to agree on, the near-strikes over salary disputes, the bad blood that lingered. He told him about the unfair evaluation system that now rated teachers based on test scores. A lady with a Frida brow—sitting at the Foreign Language table, Andrew assumed—glared at Big Brad, but he could have cared less and kept spewing.

"Don't let these fuckers fool you with the new football bleachers and freshly painted lockers," he said. "This place is rotting from the inside out." He cracked peanuts, letting the shells fall to the floor. "The social worker before you was a good guy, but he quit and took a job somewhere else. Apparently, some young chick was lined up to take the job before you, but she wised up and bowed out less than a week ago. No offense, brother."

"None taken. I'm just happy to have a job."

The bell rang. Andrew threw away half his Cuban and wished the Special Educators a good year.

"Watch your ass, Chi-cah-go," someone said. "They'll throw you under the bus in a heartbeat."

"Thanks again."

He hoped the Social Science folks were a happier bunch, but he wasn't optimistic. He lumbered back to his office and closed himself in. He scanned his bookshelf, lined with the wisdom of Jane Addams, Richard Cloward, Edith Abbott—all prominent social workers in American history. But when it came to really understanding the human condition, Paulo Coelho had become Andrew's go-to. He pulled out his wallet and read the quote he'd scribbled onto the back of a plumber's card: *When you want something, all the universe conspires to help you achieve it.*

Indeed, after everything he and Gina had been through, Clearwater was where they were supposed to be. He reminded himself of that. Water was the symbol of rebirth, of cleansing and baptism. That was all they wanted. A reset, a new beginning. He would never forget, on the night Gina miscarried, the young boy running around the hospital's waiting room in a Clearwater Beach T-shirt, the setting sun behind a row of palm trees. And after Andrew found out he was losing his job because of non-tenure and budget cuts, his barber told him he'd just returned from a paradisiacal golfing trip there. They finally made their decision to move after waking up one morning and turning on the TV to a Clearwater tourism ad: "There's a spot where the sun rises up to meet you with the morning kiss, where the sand is as soft as sugar and the water sparkles like an emerald jewel." They were on the next flight. *Always heed the omens.* That was from *The Alchemist.* A cockroach scurried across the floor, and

Andrew jumped back in surprise. Sparkling Clearwater was exactly where they needed to be.

Gina sat on the toilet seat, underwear at her ankles, pregnancy test stick between her legs. Andrew paced in the family room. The TV was on, Cubs down four runs. It was a muggy night like most, but they kept the sliding balcony door open to smell the ocean.

"Anything yet?" he said.

"I'm still trying to pee, babe. But don't get your hopes up. They say you're supposed to use morning urine for the most accurate results."

"Just try your best."

This was their new life. An apartment with a tropical ceiling fan and a lushly landscaped community pool. It was a short drive to the beach. Andrew's family questioned the move. Apart from his four years downstate for college, he'd always lived near Chicago. All his memories were laced with deep-dish pizza, bad baseball, and summer street fests. He wasn't sure he would ever get used to wearing shorts in the winter or the lizards scaling walls and racing through yards. He'd now have to endure a horrible shellfish allergy in a city where shellfish were unavoidable. For Gina, transplanting was easier. She'd been heading east ever since birth—from California to New Mexico, followed by Missouri—then moved into an apartment with Andrew on Chicago's North Side after graduating college. The bad memories in Chicago outweighed the good: an office turned into a pink baby room that could never be an office again, no matter how many coats of paint they gave it; familiar neighborhood parks teeming with kids who weren't theirs. So this was their new life and now, another pregnancy test.

Andrew heard the trickle of Gina's urine in the bowl, then a flush. She walked out with the stick, and they hovered over it, waiting in silence until two lines slowly materialized. They were unmistakably, irreversibly, solid and pink. Andrew climbed onto the couch and began jumping up and down. "I'm gonna be a daddy! Am I gonna be a daddy? I'm gonna be a daddy!"

"Maybe we shouldn't get too excited. It's early."

It was early, but so what if it was? Last time they had kept their lips sealed for twelve weeks and, still, look what happened. So why not celebrate this time? It had taken Gina almost a year to even want to try again. A crack came from the TV; Carlos Beltran hit one into the gap, sending runners in from second and third, and the Cubs were down six. Andrew grabbed her face with both hands and kissed her anyway.

"Everything's going to be fine," he said. "It was meant to happen like this. It's all falling into place. My job at the eleventh hour, this apartment. I love you."

That night, he couldn't sleep. He drove his red Volvo across the causeway to Gulf Boulevard and cruised south down the coastline past Sand Key and through the small beach towns. Windows down, half-moon above, country music (his guilty pleasure), humming. He felt energized. *When you want something, all the universe conspires to help you achieve it.* If he could get his new students to feel like that, without the drugs, without having to jump into pools from rooftops, what a gift that would be. He wondered if he'd ever need to sleep again.

By mid-morning the next day, Andrew needed a nap. On top of that, his nose was plugged and he was developing a cough. Life was good though. He opened his computer. Big Brad had included him on a mass e-mail: a YouTube clip of an overweight Indian kid in just his underwear dancing like a Bollywood superstar. "Funniest video everrr!!" was the subject. A good part of the day, Andrew had been trying to track down the other social worker on staff—Hobson, his assigned mentor. He'd stopped by his office a few times but the lights were off, blinds drawn. When he was in the faculty bathroom, hands under the sink caked in pink powdered soap, an older gentlemen emerged from the stall, tinted eyeglasses and Tom Clancy's *The Hunt for Red October* under his arm. He smelled like bad aftershave, citrusy with a hint of wood.

"Are you Hobson, by chance?" Andrew asked, only because he looked like what he imagined a Hobson would look like.

The man stared at him suspiciously like someone confronted by a lover's spouse, like he was weighing if he should clock Andrew or push him aside and run. He uttered a prolonged, "Yeah," hesitant to let it go and with a hint of a question mark as it trailed off.

Andrew introduced himself, looking at his wet, pink hands, realizing he was in no position to shake. Hobson didn't seem impressed.

"I was hoping we could split up our caseloads," Andrew said. "Do you have any time this afternoon?"

Hobson said he didn't. Said he was booked up. Said he'd call him. He brushed past Andrew without washing his hands. An hour later, Andrew got an e-mail from him with no subject. An Excel spreadsheet was attached with the names of a hundred fifty students in no particular order whom Andrew was presumably to work with. A column beside the names indicated the level of service: Individual—weekly, Social Skills Group—bi-weekly, Anger Management—as needed. Andrew wrote him back: "Great. Would you mind sharing your caseload with me too?" Hobson didn't reply.

Andrew's phone rang. He coughed into it. It was the Dean of Students. "Do you see Cole Sullivan?"

Andrew searched the spreadsheet. The name was on the list, midway down in bold with an asterisk next to it: Individual—weekly/as needed. Or in social work lingo, "as often as fucking possible." "Yes I do," Andrew said.

"Are you sick?"

"Think I got a cold."

"Well, Cole's getting suspended. We caught him with cigarettes. Not to mention he's gotten through the day wearing a shirt that says, 'I Fuck on the First Date.' We're real big on language here. Are you free to meet with him? I'll send him your way."

Andrew walked out into the hallway. His throat tickled, eyes itched. Sweat pooled under his collar from the building's heat. A boy approached, big for his age, hands like baseball gloves and a snarl that suited his face. The school's resource officer hustled close behind him. "I don't need to be escorted by some rent-a-cop," the boy said. "What do you think I'm going to do?" He feigned springing for an exit. "Psych."

"I'm Mr. Richards," Andrew said, reaching out his hand.

The boy gave him a wet noodle. "What up, yo?"

"I'm guessing you're Cole. Come into my humble abode."

Andrew closed the door to his little office. Cole sat down. Their knees almost touched.

"I should go over confidentiality before we get started," Andrew said.

"I know all about that. You can't tell anybody what we talk about unless I'm gonna blow my brains out or kill somebody."

"Essentially." His Zen fountain ran in the background like a saloon piano.

"I've been seeing shrinks since I was in fourth grade. I don't like them."

"I don't like most of them either. Rough start to the year?"

"Not really." Cole grabbed the stress ball from the table, fumbled with it.

"Look, I don't know anything about you," Andrew said. "I'm new here. So why don't you tell me about yourself before I hear it from other people."

"Like what?"

"Like where you come from, what you like to do, what makes you tick." Andrew spotted another giant cockroach crawling up the wall. Cole followed his gaze, but by then it had disappeared into the ceiling tiles.

"Well, my mom's a crazy bitch. My dad's a dick. I haven't seen the guy in like a year. I hate school. Is that what you're looking for?"

"More or less. I'm curious what you hate about school. It gets you out of the house, doesn't it?"

"I can't concentrate on any of it. Like Geometry. How am I expected to concentrate on Geometry when I've got all this shit going on in my life?"

The resource officer rapped on the door. "His mom's here to pick him up."

Andrew acknowledged him with a nod. Cole stood up. "You know, believe it or not, all life's battles teach us something," Andrew said, "even the ones we lose." That was from *The Fifth Mountain*. He considered putting his hand on Cole's shoulder, but thought better of it. "I want us to meet once a week if you're cool with that."

"Whatever, yo."

Later that afternoon, Big Brad cracked peanuts in Andrew's office, rainbow-lensed Oakleys chilling on his forehead.

"There's not a lot of direction here," Andrew said, "but I'm happy to have this job. I think I can do some good things. And my wife's pregnant."

"Congrats. How far along?"

"Just a few weeks."

"Wait 'til the second trimester. She'll be hornier than a one-eyed billy goat."

Little Napoleon interrupted with an announcement over the intercom about football practice being moved to the gym because of thunderstorms. The building groaned. "Hope everyone is having a great first week," he said, and Andrew imagined he could hear his skin sizzle. "We're happy to have the best students in Florida back with us—the future of America. And we hope you know you have the most dedicated teachers in all the state too. Have an awesome first semester. Go Tornadoes." Big Brad made the universal gesture for masturbation.

Gina had scheduled an appointment with the OB/GYN. On his way out for the day, Andrew ran into Sherri. "How's things so far?" she said, eyes about to pop, smile ready to wrap itself around her head and devour it.

"Great. Met some of my victims today."

"Just do your part, kiddo. You're not alone, all right? It takes a whole village to raise children. Any of your own yet?"

"One on the way."

"There you go then."

Andrew stopped by Hobson's office. Lights off, blinds drawn. He sniffed him out by the bathroom—the citrus and the wood. Andrew popped his head in. He hadn't gotten a good look at his outfit before, but the shabby lace-up dress shoes under the stall, the slacks pulled down to the ankles, screamed Hobson. Andrew heard a page turn. He waited outside for a minute, got a drink of water from the fountain, paced up and down the hall watching kids shove one another and hug one another and steal hats and iPods from their friends. Hobson never came out.

"You're not going anywhere," Cole's mom said. "Suspension in the first week? Strike two." She grabbed him, digging her claws into his bicep. He shoved her into the bedroom door.

"Get off me."

She scowled at him like she would scowl at his dad when he'd spit in her face or when she would confront him about a scandalous text message she'd found on his phone. "Like father, like son. Like father, like son. I'm changing the locks."

Cole grabbed her wad of keys with all its stupid key chains, like the poker chip from her Girls Weekend in Vegas and the gold bull for her zodiac sign. He ran down the stairs and slammed the front door behind him, taking off in the Hummer. She'd call his phone fifty times, threaten to bring his dad into the picture, threaten military school. He'd dare her to do something. But she'd get over it in a couple hours anyway because she'd be out on the lanai with her slutty girlfriends, drinking wine, listening to Gaga, getting ready for another night of bar hopping. Then she'd come home drunk, shake him out of bed, and ask him to have a smoke with her by the pool. At some point she'd cry about his "asshole" dad and beg him never to leave her.

Cole picked up his friends, the Polish Mafia. That's what they called themselves. Paul, Marek, and Damien. They were smoking menthols in Marek's driveway. They all looked the same: skinny, tight T-shirts, hair spiked.

"What up, wankstas?" Cole said, window down, Drake kickin', phone vibrating on the dash.

"Aw, look at you trying to flex in the Hummer." The Polish Mafia made fun of the zebra seat cover. They giggled like little girls.

Mom hated the Polish Mafia. She said Cole had changed ever since becoming friends with them. She said he was a perfect kid, an "A" student, before they started coming around. Total bullshit. The Polish Mafia liked hanging out at Cole's house because he had PS3 on a wide screen, the biggest pool of anyone in their squad, and a foosball table. Mom thought they were stealing stuff from the house. Any time twenty bucks or a pair of earrings went missing, she blamed the Polish Mafia. She said they were using him because his family had money. At three A.M., though, wasted and cross-eyed, she was all about sharing her cigarettes and unloading her grief on them. At three A.M. they were her best friends for life. BF4L.

It was Marek's idea to get high and egg cars at the beach. He got the urge every few months. He rode shotgun. They cruised down Mandalay, lined with palm trees, past surf shops and T-shirt emporiums. Paul climbed over Cole's shoulder to yell out the window at girls with sarongs wrapped over bikinis and couples dining at outdoor cafés. His knees pushed against the back of the seat. "Yo, I'm trying to drive," Cole said. His phone vibrated for the tenth time.

They picked up a carton of eggs at the Pick Kwik. In the North Beach lot, they launched them at the nicest rides they could find: a Ferrari F12, a Porsche Boxster, some old dude's Jaguar. Between tosses, Marek was on his phone trying to find out where the party was. Damien kept turning, looking out the back window, for cops or good Samaritans calling 911. Cole didn't care. A part of him was daring to get caught. Daring his dad to come and try beating his ass now that he was bigger. Daring to be sent away. He whipped the last egg at a Benzo.

"Your mom's going to be pissed," Marek said, cackling.

"Fuck her."

Cole went home at the end of the night only because he had nowhere else to crash. His mom got home after him with a bag of chili cheese fries, smelling like cigarettes and booze. Her eyes rolled. She grinned.

"I should kill you," she said.

"But you won't."

Outside, she lit two smokes and gave him one. Frogs croaked. The underwater lights illuminated the kidney-shaped pool, first green, then purple, then red.

"You know how much trouble you'd be in if I called the cops?" she said. "Stolen car. Driving without a license."

"Whatever. Why didn't you?"

"'Cause I love you, you little shit."

"No you don't."

"Oh come here." She hugged him. Buried his face into her.

"All right, all right, I love you too, Mom," he mumbled. "I love you too."

It was just before Winter Break when the buzz started. Sherri stormed into her office with puffy eyes and slammed the door shut. Her weight had slowly been coming back, filling in like an inflatable tube. The Special Educators broke the news at the cafeteria table. The school district was in a hole, a giant hole, like a fifty-five million dollar one. It was no secret falling property taxes had been cutting into the budget. The district had been tapping federal stimulus money and reserve funds to make ends meet. That could only last so long.

Dee, the older woman with the necktie, which was now inadvertently resting in the sauce of her Mediterranean-style grouper, leaned in toward the middle of the table and spoke in a hush. "You just knew they were going to rock the classroom at some point."

Little Napoleon darted into the cafeteria. Short people always looked like they were walking fast. "Shhh," someone said, "Rice Dick is coming through."

He glanced at Big Brad as he passed, hands in pockets. "Hiya, Bob."

Big Brad nodded. "Fucking guy doesn't even know my name. You believe this?"

"So you're saying they're going to cut jobs?" Andrew said. The table turned to him, eyes down, no answer. "Well that can't be good for me."

The state increase in teacher pay and higher enrollment wouldn't help. Even without the budget cuts, all new Florida hires were on annual contracts and a merit-based pay system. Sink or swim. Motivate some of the worst-paid teachers in America.

"You'll be fine, Coach," Big Brad said. "You work with the crazies. They're not going to get rid of the guy who works with the crazies. Plus you got your hands in all kinds of pots."

"I just have to keep doing my thing. Stay focused."

A Warrior cannot lower his head, otherwise he loses sight of the horizon of his dreams. Yeah, *Warrior of the Light.* Each day with his morning coffee, Andrew would sit for ten minutes on his patio visualizing their future life, trying to burn it into reality: school football games with the family, weeknight sunsets on the beach, kid stumbling through the sand. No village, just them. He had steered his destiny. In the past few months, he had volunteered to be the Asian Club sponsor, despite knowing little about Asian culture aside from what he'd learned from briefly dating a Vietnamese girl in college. He became the Gymnastics coach because that's what the universe had dropped in his lap. He took on the Chess Team too. Gina complained he was never home, that she was tired, that she needed help. "I'm doing this for us," he said. "You think I like staying up all night trying to figure out how to teach a back handspring?"

After lunch, Andrew went to his office and flipped through his schedule. Back-to-back students all afternoon. He never turned anyone away. It hadn't taken long to realize Hobson had dumped the most difficult cases on him. A girl whose father had been locked up for child porn. A boy whose dad lit himself on fire outside his mistress's house. Another kid whose mom accidentally ran over his little brother in the driveway. And there was Cole, oddly his favorite, who didn't go a day without getting into some kind of trouble: swearing, fighting, cutting, stealing, lying, being. Hobson, on the contrary, spent his days between the faculty bathroom and talking to parents about fostering good homework habits.

Andrew's office was hot and sticky, but that's how it was every Monday. Most mornings too. To save money, the school would turn off the A/C after three P.M. and on weekends. Andrew found a dead cockroach, legs up, next to the floor lamp. He was convinced his office was infested with them. He'd often find droppings under his desk or their brown, empty cases behind the bookshelf. The janitors had put out baits and traps, insecticides in cracks and crevices. But just when he thought they were gone, he'd spot one in the morning scurrying into the wall as the lights went on. And there was the smell—the musty smell that never went away.

Before his next appointment, Andrew stopped in to see Sherri. She'd been getting bigger and sadder, her mouth starting to collapse under her cheeks. Andrew caught her walking into her office. He coughed into his sleeve.

"You sick?" she asked.

He felt awful every day. Stuffy nose. Skin rashes. Wheezing. "The doctor can't find anything wrong with me. I'm supposed to go see a specialist, but it's kind of hard to fit anything in between Gymnastics practice and OB/GYN visits."

She nodded, then heard her phone ring and moaned.

"Hey, listen, are you okay?" Andrew said. "Do you want to talk?"

She pointed to the picture of the canoe, now hanging crooked on her wall. "Just gotta keep paddling, kiddo, right? Take to the oars." She forced a smile and closed the door behind her.

Before heading home for Christmas, they had their twenty-week ultrasound. Gina lay flat on the table. The nurse rubbed gel on her growing belly, a dark line running down it like a skid mark. "Oooh, that's cold," she said. Andrew held her hand.

It took all he had to keep from falling back into that dark place. To smother the fear clamoring to be let out. The fear that when the wand was placed onto her belly, the heart wouldn't beat. The fear that the universe wasn't conspiring on their behalf after all since it obviously hadn't the last time. Where was Paulo Coelho a year ago? He tried shaking it off, cherishing the moment, because it was wrong to take it away from this child. This child that could be, that would be. He knew Gina was fighting the fear too, worse than him, so he rubbed her knuckles, kept on a big plastic smile, made wisecracks. "I wonder if you'll be able to see the giant cheeseburger Gina wolfed down before we got here."

The ultrasound tech put the wand on Gina's belly and glided it across her skin, up and down the hump. Gina was silent. She stared at Andrew. He stared back, stuck out his tongue, kept smiling, rubbed. A newborn wailed from another room. The tech finally pointed at the screen. "There's your little one," she said. "Head's there. Spine. Looks like a railroad track. And there's the heart beating. You can hear it. Sounds perfect."

Baboom, baboom, baboom, baboom. Andrew exhaled and fixated on the tiny heart flickering.

"Do you want to know the baby's sex?" the tech said.

They looked at each other. "Sure," they said in unison.

"I'm searching between the little legs for something. Yup, I see boy parts. It's a boy. It's definitely a boy, guys. Congratulations."

"Oh my God," Gina said. "It's a boy."

Back in the Midwest, in snow boots and wool hats, they spent a few days with Gina's parents and a few with his. Late night under the Christmas tree with everyone else asleep, Andrew's mom asked him if they'd thought about moving back to Chicago.

"We like Florida," he said.

"Do you? Or is it just too hard to be here?"

She reminded him how difficult it was raising a kid, especially with full-time jobs and no family around. "It takes a village," she said. "We can help you."

He hugged her, kissed her wrinkled forehead. "Thanks, Mom. We'll be all right, though, I promise. We'll figure it out."

He crawled into his old twin bed, beside his high school diploma on the wall and the dresser stacked with baseball trophies and model cars. He pressed against Gina and put his hand on her belly. The little man was probably asleep too, but Andrew tapped his finger lightly against her, hoping he'd give a kick back.

"Did you see your dad on Christmas?" Andrew asked Cole over the whir of the fan.

"Nope. He texted me."

"Did you respond?"

"Fuck no."

From the outside, the kid was well put together. He'd grown six inches since the start of the year. He was shaving. His bronze biceps strained his sleeves every time his arms bent. Looked as much a man as Andrew. He was a big oak, rotting from the inside out.

"You never told me what happened the last time you saw your dad," Andrew said.

"The last time I saw my dad, me and my mom walked in on him banging one of his hookers. Then my mom tried driving off in his Benz so he pulled her out by her hair and beat the living shit out of her. That's the last time I saw him. And my mom was begging me to call him on Christmas. Do you believe that? 'Call your dad,' she kept telling me."

"How did that make you feel?"

"She's fuckin' cray. Why would I listen to her? After everything he's done, she won't even divorce the bastard. Probably because he still pays for all the expensive crap we've got. She's that pathetic."

Two teachers chatted outside Andrew's office. Their voices were muffled but he made out buzzwords like "Little Napoleon," "narcissist," "demoralizing." Cole sat back with his ankles crossed. Andrew leaned in toward him and lowered his voice.

"I understand why you're angry with your parents, I do. But you're the one who's going to have to live with the consequences of your actions. You failed all but one class first semester." Andrew raised his index finger and shook it for emphasis. "The school wants to do an evaluation and put you in Special Ed. for an Emotional/Behavioral Disability. Is that what you want for yourself?"

"Whatever, yo." Cole unzipped his backpack and pulled out his Beats.

"I know you don't mean that."

"I do. Nobody can make me do shit. I won't show up."

Before lunch, Andrew called Cole's mom from his desk. He dreaded those calls. He reached for the framed 3D ultrasound photo and brought it closer. His screen saver popped on, a frozen Lake Michigan rolling out to the Chicago skyline. Cole's mom answered. Her voice was raspy; a cough loosened the phlegm.

"I'm sorry if I woke you," Andrew said.

"I'm a realtor. I make my own schedule. What did that little shit say to you now?"

"The bottom line is we're doing all we can here to help him, but he's still struggling. He avoids doing any work. He's constantly roaming the halls. When he's in class, his language is horrendous. And you know how much we stress appropriate language here."

"So what do you want me to do about it? I ground him. I yell at him. I take away his video games. He doesn't listen to me."

"Have you ever considered family therapy?"

Andrew could hear her take a long pull from her cigarette. "Please, we don't need that, okay? No family's perfect. Cole's biggest problem is he's lazy. And spoiled. Kid's got everything you could want. He's got nothing to be rebelling over."

"With all due respect, my professional opinion is there's more to it than that."

"Andy. Can I call you Andy? Do you have any kids?"

"No, well, not yet. A little one on the way."

She laughed; her phlegm rattled. "Do me a favor and call me when you have a teenager then, okay? You'll see for yourself. They've got minds of their own."

That afternoon, Big Brad sat in Andrew's office slurping down a Diet Coke Big Gulp. He cracked peanuts.

"Hey man, be careful with the peanut shells, will ya?" Andrew said. "I'm really trying to keep this place as unappealing to the roaches as possible."

Andrew told Big Brad about Cole. Big Brad said kids like that were hopeless. They ended up in jail or dead. Andrew argued he was only fifteen. He was actually pretty sharp. He had his whole life ahead of him and, believe it or not, had let his guard down once and admitted wanting to be a cop or lawyer when he grew up. Big Brad scoffed.

"All the dipshits want to be cops or lawyers when they grow up." Through the door crack, they saw Hobson pass, shoes squeaking, hardcover under his arm.

"See, that guy's got it made, Coach," Big Brad said. "They can't touch him with his seniority. While you're slaving away hoping not to get laid off, he's spending his days on the shitter, collecting a paycheck."

Big Brad reached around the fake palm tree and closed the door, which usually meant he wanted to talk about young teachers he wished he could bang. Big Brad was on a long-term contract.

"C'mon, tell me about your break," Andrew said.

"Break? It sucked. Took the kids to Disney for like the tenth time. Stood in lines like an idiot all week." He pulled out his phone and showed Andrew a picture of himself, the family, Winnie the Pooh and Tigger as bookends, at the Splash Mountain exit. "I guess that's what dads do though, right?"

Cole ambled into Spanish class one morning, hat on his head, books against his hip. He was wearing his pajama pants, hair matted to his forehead. He crossed the threshold just as the Taylor Swift passing period song cut out and the bell rang. "Take off the hat, Señor Sullivan," his teacher said. "You know the rules."

He rolled his eyes. He was pulling a seven percent in there. She was pissed because he was bringing her average down. She was pissed because she was old and ugly too. She took him aside.

"I'm glad you decided to join us," she said. "But where have you been the last four days?"

Behind Arby's. In my basement playing video games. Couldn't she just appreciate he showed up? *I was with those fuckers,* Cole wanted to say, nodding to the Polish Mafia as they passed, late to class themselves. "Ahhh, busted!" They cackled. Cole flipped them off.

"Let's keep moving, guys," his teacher said. She glared at them. They weren't trippin'. "So what's your explanation? *¿Dónde has estado?*"

He didn't know what that meant. He avoided making eye contact, shrugged his shoulders. "I don't know."

"You don't know?" He didn't answer. She waited. "Do you even care if you pass my class?"

These were the triggers his shrink talked about. He was supposed to count to ten now. Take deep breaths. Visualize himself on an island beach. He was supposed to shut up and care about her class even though she didn't give two shits about him. *Teachers hate kids,* Cole would say. His shrink would tell him he was overgeneralizing. "See, this is why I hate coming to class. Because I have to get harassed every day about not doing my homework or not being here or wearing my hat. It's bullshit."

"Take some responsibility for your actions, Señor Sullivan. You're a young man now."

"Screw this. I'm outta here." He put his hat back on and marched toward the stairs.

"I'm calling security," she said.

"Whatever."

As he walked out the doors, he saw the rent-a-cop running down the hallway, keys jingling, huffing into his walkie talkie. The guy was going to have a heart attack. Cole started trotting, jogging at best, because he knew the loser would never catch up to him. He cut behind the football bleachers, over the fence, and darted between cars across Gulf to Bay Boulevard. He lit a smoke in the shopping center lot and kept walking. It wasn't long before his mom was blowing up his phone. He ignored the first ten calls and her text messages: "Pick up the damn phone NOW!!!" She called again.

"What?" he said.

"Where the hell are you? The school called me."

"Nowhere."

"Get your ass back to school or home, I swear."

"Okay."

"What else did you do, huh?" she said. "Why don't you tell me? The cops came by this morning. Were you egging cars from my Hummer again, which you should never have been driving in the first place? What, with your stupid little loser friends I told you not to hang out with? Do you know how much trouble I can be in? Strike three, you little shit. You're out."

"Whatever." He hung up.

Andrew knocked on Sherri's office doorframe. "I have an important appointment this afternoon," he said. "Is it okay if I leave a little early?"

She glanced up at him, then went back to playing with her cell phone. "Yeah, sure, whatever you gotta do, kiddo."

Sherri had buzzed her hair and taken down most of the posters and framed art from her walls. The room was bare. "It just doesn't feel right keeping 'em up," she'd said. Her Zulu tattoo had grown illegible, stretching across her ballooning calf. The sun on her shoulder blade was now swelling into a fiery red giant, forecasting the Earth's demise.

The job cuts were imminent after all. At best, Sherri would have to lose staff. Good, young, enthusiastic staff she'd helped hire, helped mentor. If the rumors were true, though, she'd be gone too with a handful of other department heads. They'd be replaced by cheaper lead teachers. By robots, by more of Little Napoleon's cronies. Divide and conquer.

The night before, parents and students had protested at a school board meeting. The board was considering cutting two hundred teachers, guidance counselors, library specialists, secretaries, teacher assistants, and others. New staff would perish first. Last ones in, first ones out. The future of education, the future of America down a sinkhole. Andrew was leaving school late after a chess meet in which his boys bravely fell 5-63. The crowd was marching through the parking lot holding up picket signs, chanting, "Save our teachers" and "What about our kids?" and "*Sí se puede.*"

Andrew looked out Sherri's window at the "Wet Paint" signs taped onto lockers. Curiously, the building had been in the midst of a massive makeover. Everything was being re-painted in crimson and gray—the school colors—from the bleachers to bathroom stalls. Old, rustic wood walls along hallways with their knots and dings and history were replaced with new, shiny faux paneling. Janitors were working overtime. "We need more school spirit here," Little Napoleon was going around preaching. State-of-the-art LED TVs were being erected around the building, running round-the-clock clips of pep assemblies, sports highlights, and choir concerts. Little Napoleon made broadcasts each morning inviting students to various school events ("Come out and bring your swag!") he never showed up to himself. He wore makeup for his broadcasts. He filmed them next to a dusty American flag with frayed edges. He was growing a weak goatee. The Special Educators sat around the cafeteria table calculating how many careers were killed for those TVs.

Still, the staff had a chance at heroism, at saving lives, saving America. The union put it to a vote. Everyone could sacrifice a cut in pay in exchange for at least some jobs or let fate run its course. They voted unanimously to keep their pay.

"Hear anything about the social workers yet?" Andrew asked Sherri.

She kept playing with her phone. "Not yet. You should be okay though. The world will always have people with problems. Just keep doing your part, saving America's youth."

That afternoon, Andrew sat in the allergist's office talking history with the nurse.

"I've always been allergic to shellfish," he said. "My throat starts tickling the minute I walk into a seafood restaurant."

The nurse pricked his arms with various allergens: mold, pollen, peanuts, seafood, mollusks, crustaceans, cats. Within minutes, different spots started lighting up, inflaming, itching. Numbers two, seven, eight, twelve. Christ. He waited, staring at pictures on the walls of sinus cavities and people sneezing in fields of ragweed and sunflowers. The doctor knocked and came in. She had an elephant pin on her lab coat that read, "No peanuts. I'm allergic."

"What's the verdict?" Andrew said.

"Well, you're definitely allergic to shellfish. You're allergic to cockroaches too. They have the same major allergen, a muscle protein called tropomyosin, if you want to get technical, so a lot of people who are allergic to one react to the other as well."

"You've got to be kidding me."

The doctor cleaned Andrew's arms. "Nope. Why, been around many roaches lately?"

Swarms of love bugs crashed against Andrew's Volvo as he drove home. It was spring and they'd descended onto Florida. They invaded twice a year. For weeks, his coworkers had been warning him to coat his car. Dee swore by PAM cooking spray for the nose and mirrors, Big Brad by baby oil for the hood, grill, and bumper. Andrew never got around to it. Carcasses of the little black and white bugs were now crusted across his windshield. "You gotta wash that shit off ASAP too, Coach," Big Brad had cautioned, "or it'll start eating the paint."

At a red light with the A/C blasting and country music twanging, Gina called. "I haven't felt him move all afternoon," she said. "I'm scared."

"I'm sure he's fine. He's probably in a food coma. Did you eat turkey for lunch again?"

The third trimester had so far been brutal. Backaches, swollen ankles, and hemorrhoids. There was the anxiety and the mood swings. Gina would sob to episodes of *Keeping Up with the Kardashians*, laugh hysterically any time the E*TRADE talking baby commercials came on. Big Brad called it Third Trimester Freak-Out Syndrome.

She was petrified of getting listeriosis from contaminated food, made Andrew barbeque meat until it was bone dry, avoided processed lunchmeats and soft cheeses ("Is that Brie in this sandwich? There's Brie in this sandwich!"). She suspected gestational diabetes anytime she felt thirsty. But Gina never complained of the little man not moving. If anything, she complained of him kicking too hard, worried he'd crack one of her ribs. So Andrew buzzed home, hand on his horn, rolling through stop signs.

Gina was pacing at the door when he got there. "We need to go to the doctor."

Back on the OB/GYN's table, hair fanning from her head, Gina held back tears. Her lower lip quivered. Andrew smiled, rubbed her knuckles, kissed her forehead.

"Something's wrong, Andrew," she said. She stared at him without blinking.

"Everything's okay, honey, trust me. You're worrying yourself sick for nothing."

Andrew's fear tried crawling back in, but it was no match anymore for the dream. They'd look back on this and laugh. They'd laugh at this just like they'd laugh at the time during the second trimester when Gina bent down to pray and farted in church or when she sneezed and wet her pants at the movies. They'd laugh while they sat on the beach watching the sunset, the little man stumbling through the sand.

The doctor greeted them with handshakes and said, "So what's going on?" with a little grin that read, *You poor, overemotional woman in your third trimester with those rollercoaster hormones*. Andrew winked at him. Gina shared her concerns, and the doc said, "We'll take a listen," and pressed the Doppler against her bump. There was the familiar whooshing like the inside of a conch shell, nothing more. He hopped from one spot to another, but still nothing. No beating, no pounding to be let out. "He's probably curled into a ball," the doctor said. "Hiding from me." But his grin was gone. *Don't give in to your fears.*

The tech came in and lubed Gina's belly. The womb lit up the screen, patterns changing, a kaleidoscope as the wand moved across her abdomen. She found the little man's face. Nose, lips, chin. "There he is," Andrew said. Gina craned her neck to see. The tech clicked buttons on the keyboard. She looked at the doctor. They seemed to be communicating something awful with their eyes. They didn't speak.

"What's happening?" Gina said. "What is it?"

The doctor ran his hand through his hair, exhaled, then bent down to sit beside Gina.

"No," Andrew whispered. He felt the dream tearing away from his head and chest and down his limbs, out from his tingling fingers. The room began to spin and the last thing he remembered before blacking out was the doctor putting his hand on Gina's arm, the muffled sound of her repeating, "No, no, no, no, no," and the doctor saying, "I'm so sorry, sweetie. There's no heartbeat."

Cole cruised by the house. His mom wasn't home yet. He slid into the basement, lit a smoke, and played *Dead Space* on the big screen. He was using a plasma cutter, wasting necromorphs, when he heard the front door slam shut. Keys clanked onto the marble counter, then footsteps stomped through the kitchen, into the bedroom and bathrooms. The basement door swung open. The footsteps marched closer. He kept playing.

"You think you're a real tough guy now, don't you?" Cole spun around. It was his dad. An Infector took advantage and pounced him, jab after jab from its talon booming over the surround sound.

Cole tried standing his ground, showing he wasn't afraid, but he'd seen his dad move like that before. With purpose, crazy in his eyes, sweat on his balding head. He'd seen him move like that all his life: at his mom, at umpires, at cops. So he dropped the controller and shuffled around the leather couch.

"C'mere. What do you think I'm gonna do? C'mere."

Cole let up. He kept his shoulder turned to shield his face, his knee bent to run if he had to. It didn't help. When his dad was within arm's reach, he cracked him upside the head. The cigarette fell to the tile, still lit. Cole's ear rang. His dad twisted his arm behind his back.

"You're smoking in my house?"

"Whatever, yo." And another crack, this time to the lip, busting it open.

"You don't fuckin' 'yo' your father. Who do you think you're talking to?" He dug his nails into Cole's neck and dragged him up the stairs. "Where does your mom keep the trash bags?" He flung open cabinet doors that snapped back like overextended joints. If Mom was home, there'd be a brawl over that for sure and Cole would've taken advantage and bounced. Where the hell was she anyway? His dad finally found the bags in the pantry, tossing boxes of pasta and cereal onto the floor. He yanked one out. "Grab your shit. You're moving in with me. Whatever fits in this bag is all you get."

He pulled Cole through the hallway, banging him against the walls, knocking down old wedding photos and family vacation shots. "I ain't going anywhere with you, man," Cole said. And another smack to the jaw. A pop to the temple.

"Fine, then I'll pick your shit out for you." He grabbed wrinkled T-shirts and boxers from the floor, threw them into the bag. He crumpled an empty pack of smokes from the dresser and tried shoving it in Cole's mouth. He hauled him out of the house toward his black Escalade. Cole's bare feet burned on the pavement. He worked to pry himself away, but his dad's grip only got tighter, nastier. He propped his foot against the side of the car to keep from getting forced in. More chops to the back of the neck. A woman walking her dog gasped and then hurried off.

His dad's hand was getting sweaty, sliding down his arm, losing its grip on his neck. Cole took another crack to the eye and could feel it swell. The weight of his dad pressed his ribs into the door frame. He writhed and flailed and kicked until his dad couldn't hang on or didn't bother to anymore or figured he'd gotten his point across. When he broke loose, he took off running.

"You got no place to go, son," his dad said. "You're running for nothing."

By then Cole was halfway down the block, arms and legs heavy, eye throbbing. Even when he turned the corner, his chest heaving, lungs burning, he could still hear his dad hollering: "You got no place to go."

Andrew and Gina's baby boy was delivered that night. Six pounds, twelve ounces. He had ten fingers and ten toes, dark hair. Hello and goodbye all in one breath. The explanation was it was an umbilical cord accident. A rare occurrence. A one-in-two-hundred pregnancies occurrence. The cord had somehow become knotted, cutting off oxygen to their little man. "Plenty of people go through this," the doctor said, "and go on to have big, beautiful families. I know it's hard to think about now, but if that's what you two want don't let this stop you from trying."

It was three A.M. and Gina was asleep in the hospital bed, tubes running from her arms, various machines beeping and humming. Andrew couldn't get comfortable in the cot they'd given him. It was too small, too cold, too hard, too real, and he wasn't ready to admit any of it was real because it wasn't part of the dream. He paced the dimly lit hallways past the nurses' station, sleepy as an all-night diner. He needed to go for a drive.

His Volvo was still crusted with love bugs. After days of baking under the sun, their acid had started leaving pits and etches all over the hood. He had never cared about anything less. He wouldn't care if they ate through its flesh, down to its bones. If they came back to life and carried it away. Andrew drove to the school, maybe because it was the closest thing he had to home out there. Why was it whenever communities had tragedies, people always gathered around schools? He parked in the empty south lot, turned off his ignition, and cried for the first time. The school understood. The school gave him comfort. The football field, bleachers, tennis courts, flagpole, cockroaches, crickets all hung over his shoulders, swallowed him.

Andrew collected himself when he heard a noise: feet shuffling across the pavement, the rattle of the chain-link fence. He looked into the rearview and saw a tall figure approaching, shirtless and barefoot, staggering. Andrew recognized him. It was Cole. He turned the ignition, thought about leaving, put the car in reverse. He didn't want to be seen. He didn't want anybody else's problems. But then he watched Cole bend over and hurl, and he got out of the car.

"Hey Cole, you okay? It's me, Mr. Richards."

When he got closer, Andrew could see parts of his face were puffy and bruised. He was pale, eyes vacant, pupils big as nickels. He stared through Andrew and swayed. "Yooo, Mr. Richards," he finally slurred. "That palm tree is following me. I think we should go to your office next period."

The lamppost lit him up like a Broadway lead. He was having a substance-induced psychotic episode. Maybe a mixture of too much alcohol and pot. Maybe worse. There were too many stories of intoxicated youth falling and drowning in pools or stumbling into traffic.

"Do you have your phone on you?" Andrew said.

"Uh…" he patted his shirtless chest for pockets.

"Why don't you hop in the car, buddy?"

"Totes. This your new office? It's sick, bro."

They drove in silence, windows down. Andrew turned on the country music station and handed Cole a bottled water.

"What happened to your face?"

"My dad showed up and beat the shit out of me," Cole said in an apparent moment of clarity. His head bobbed.

"Stay awake, pal."

They floated down Gulf to Bay through green lights. The breeze whirled doctor's papers around the backseat.

"Dude, you're the only guy who actually gives a crap about kids at this school. I'm gonna get my shit together for you. I'm gonna run for class president, yo. Haha." Cole took a swig of water and it dribbled down his chin and onto his bony chest. He stuck his head out the window and let the wind tousle his hair. He was just a kid. "So where we going anyway?" he asked.

"We're taking a little trip to the Morton Plant Hospital," Andrew said. "We're going to get you checked out."

When Andrew returned to work several days later, he was called down to the principal's office. It was his first time in there. Little Napoleon sat behind his mahogany desk, slouched back in his black leather chair, legs crossed, but like a woman, a fairly typical principal's posture. The desktop was lined with expensive fountain pens. Sherri was there too. Her ass now hung over either side of the chair. All that was left of her face were two bulging eyes and a mound of flesh. She stared at the ground. Andrew eyed the picture hanging behind Little Napoleon, a tiny baby hand nestled into an adult palm that read, "INTEGRITY. We Make a Living by What We Get. We Make a Life by What We Give."

"Any idea why you're in here, Andy?" Little Napoleon said.

Andrew wanted to believe he'd be given a sympathy card, a bouquet of chrysanthemums, a shoulder to cry on. He'd lost ten pounds. He was pale and weak. By Little Napoleon's tone, Andrew knew better.

"Um…"

"Cole Sullivan's mom called me a few days ago, infuriated, threatening to sue," Little Napoleon said. "She told me you picked him up in your car one night and drove him to the hospital. Said you called the police and DCF with some story about how his dad beat him up."

"Holy crow," Sherri uttered.

"Yeah, that's all accurate," Andrew said, "except the part about it being story."

Little Napoleon spun in his chair, arms folded, looked up at nothing in particular, and let out a condescending laugh. Like a Joe Biden laugh. "Allowing a student into your car, Andy, is highly—*highly*—inappropriate, and it puts the district in quite a predicament legally. You must know that, right?"

"With all due respect, what was I supposed to do? Leave him there?"

"Yes."

"What if he died?"

"Not your responsibility. Or ours either, for that matter. He wasn't on our watch."

"I reacted," Andrew said. "I did what I felt was right."

"Well, it was wrong. I spoke with the superintendent. We're going to have to suspend you while we investigate the matter."

"You're kidding me."

"If you choose to resign, that may save us all some headaches. This could get ugly. I'll write you a letter of recommendation. You decide."

"What about the students I work with, the clubs I sponsor?"

"Good question. We'll need all hands on deck." Little Napoleon closed his eyes for a second, then shot them open and pointed to Sherri. "What's his name—Hobson—can coordinate our efforts, right? Isn't he our head social worker?"

"Yes, uh-huh," Sherri said. "I can talk to him." She jotted down a reminder. *Contact Hobson re: damage control*, Andrew read from her lap.

Andrew stared out the floor-to-ceiling windows at the courtyard. It was bathed in sunshine. There were mango trees, songbirds, and tropical plants. How great it would be, Andrew thought, to have a view like that every day. The best view in the building. It was no wonder Little Napoleon never left his office.

A giant moon was beginning to burn its image into the sky. Andrew and Gina sat on the beach gazing into the Gulf, seaweed against their feet. Storm clouds were moving in. Seagulls circled and squawked overhead, then skirted across the sand to pick up leftover cigarette butts and potato chips. Waves broke as they reached the shore.

"We're all alone again," Gina said, her eyes welling with tears. "We have nothing to lose anymore."

Andrew pulled her in closer. "You'll always have me." His love would be all hers if that's the way it had to be.

His mom's voice echoed in his ears, pleading for them to stop the nonsense, to come back home already to their family and friends. Maybe that was the right idea.

The last few beachgoers collected umbrellas and towels as the first drops of rain began to fall. Andrew stared at the sand and pictured their lost children, a boy and girl, stomping in the pools starting to form, leaving vanishing footprints, laughing at the castles turning into mudslides. *When I had nothing to lose, I had everything. Eleven Minutes.* He never understood what that meant. He waited for the sea to pick them up and drag them in, for it to have its way.

Andrew's reinstatement came unceremoniously a few weeks later via an e-mail from Little Napoleon. He was unshaven at the kitchen table, drinking coffee, hunting for jobs. "I'm going back to work, honey," he said.

At school, he found an unsealed envelope in his mailbox with a letter:

The Board of Education of Clearwater School District 264 has approved the continuation of your contract for the 2014-15 school year.

He read on. The excitement was short-lived.

"I've been reassigned to Clearwater Elementary next year," he told Big Brad as they bowled through the crowded hall, a mess of backpacks and ear buds. Taylor Swift sang of breakups and heartache, of failed love. The sound of lockers slamming and students complaining about exams and prom dates and summer jobs all ran together, rumbled.

"That's bullshit, Coach," Big Brad said. "That's just Rice Dick trying to show you who's boss."

"Maybe it'll be all right."

Andrew heard Cole coming before he saw him. At the end of the hallway, he and the Polish Mafia were pushing and shoving, preserving their reputation as the loudest and most obnoxious kids in the school. Andrew had been forbidden to counsel Cole any longer. He nodded to him and pulled him aside.

"Hey Mr. R., sorry about my crazy-ass mom. She was pissed for about a week then forgot about it like she always does. "

"No reason to apologize. You okay?"

"I'm cool. Got a restraining order on my asshole dad. And it looks like I'm going to military school next year after all. My mom's got some meetings lined up."

"How do you feel about that?"

"It's all right, I guess. I heard you work out there every day, so at least I can get ripped."

The better bet was Mom would pull the plug on it. Cole would be right back in school there come August. His dad would be in his life again before long. The kid would eventually have to fight the waves or sink. Or sink trying to fight the waves.

"I hope everything works out for you one way or another," Andrew said.

"I'll come back to see you, yo."

"I'm actually being transferred to the elementary school."

"No, for real? That sucks. You're like the only cool person in this school."

"Be well, buddy."

When Andrew got to his office, Sherri's framed picture of the empty canoe on the shore rested against his door. There was a post-it on it: *Keep paddling, kiddo—S.* He looked for her, but she wasn't in sight. He dragged the picture into his room; it was heavier than he'd thought. When he flipped the light on, there were no cockroaches to greet him, no cockroaches scuttling back home. He peeked under his desk. The dead bodies, the feces, the egg cases—they were all gone too. He turned on the Zen fountain and checked his schedule. He breathed in, exhaled, and waited for the next appointment, the next young life he'd do his best to save.

HOLD ON

Ethan's virtual shrink said this would be good for him. It's his first time in a human touch center, even though they've been popping up across America since the late 2030s. *A place to feel connected in a disconnected world.* It's not that he hasn't wanted to go before. On the contrary, he's been curious for years. As his shrink says, the first step is always the hardest.

His half-hour cuddle session is with a woman named Ava, the touch specialist he's chosen from the digital catalog. Her blue hair had jumped out at him. She reminded him of a young Katy Perry, his childhood crush, a sexy spitfire from many moons ago.

They lie in the warmth of a sleep pod, both clothed, Ethan embracing Ava in the spoon position. His fully erect penis pokes her in the back, a no-no in human touch centers, but it makes him feel alive. And thankfully she's a good sport about it. "Thanks for not giving me a hard time," Ethan says, "no pun intended." Because really it's not a sexual thing, even though she's an attractive woman and her hair smells like blueberries and he would have sex with her, no questions asked, if it were that sort of thing. *Dead puppies and grandmas*, Ethan repeats to himself, *dead puppies and grandmas*.

The last time Ethan held another person close was at his father's funeral. Aunt Linda pressed against him, sobbing on his black sport coat, Uncle Paul suffocating him in a bear hug. He reminisces about them while lulled by the sound of logs crackling on a campfire, waves slapping the shore.

"I saw you guys are hiring," Ethan says to Ava.

"Yeah, we can use some extra bodies around here."

The time projects against the wall of the pod. Five minutes left. Ethan squeezes Ava, smells her hair, holds on. He fantasizes about the old days. About his folks and Claire, of course. About birthdays and bar mitzvahs and graduation parties.

Ethan's shrink is in his living room, but not really. She's a holographic projection. Cropped hair, cream cardigan, sitting cross-legged on a purple sofa. Her name is Sandy. There are sensors tracking and analyzing Ethan's facial expressions, body language, subtle gestures, shifts in eye contact.

"How are you, Ethan?" Sandy says.

"Still trying to figure out why I bother waking up every morning, but better."

"Have you thought about taking your life?"

"Not lately, no."

It's easy to blame the Superbug, the terrorist-made virus that swept through the Americas and wiped out a tenth of Milwaukee, but really Ethan's downward spiral began before that. When Claire left him. At the time, he knew she'd be the only woman he'd ever be with but didn't want to believe it. His parents died shortly thereafter.

Ethan works from home; his company doesn't even have an office. His groceries get delivered weekly and entertainment is at his fingertips. Except for his teeth, which he's sorely neglected, there's no reason to leave the apartment anymore.

"You can keep doing what you're doing and feel miserable," Sandy says, "or you can extend your comfort zone and see if it rewards you."

"Why does it matter?"

"Because the Earth hasn't burst into a fiery ball just yet."

Ethan begins moonlighting at the touch center on weekday mornings. Off-peak hours. He robo-cabs it there and back alone. Still, working there is a leap from the isolation of his apartment, and it's the first time he's felt inspired in years. He knows he's not handsome by conventional standards, but he can give a mean hug and they never have enough guys to work at places like this anyway.

He burns through fifteen hours of training. Safety, appropriate conduct and behavior, promotion and marketing. There's science behind it. *Cuddling releases oxytocin. Oxytocin feels good. Oxytocin builds intimacy.*

Most patrons are women. Single, corporate, Type A. In and out. Ethan gets his first male client on a Wednesday, and he reeks of skunk. He recognizes him as soon as he crawls into the pod.

"Tyler?"

"Ethan! Get the hell outa here." From the pod speakers, humpback whales moan as they migrate out of the Norwegian Sea.

Ethan and Tyler were neighbors as kids. Played backyard football on summer nights until it was too dark to see the ball and video games late into winter nights well after they were supposed to be in bed. They went to school together too, like *school* school. Back in the day when people had to enter buildings to be educated. Tyler's hair is now wiry and gray and pulled back into a pony tail. His face is fuller and two distinct shades, a lighter strip across the eyes where his sunglasses have kept his skin from cooking. He is an inverted raccoon.

"How long has it been?" Tyler asks. "Since high school?"

"Somewhere thereabouts."

"Wow, so you're working here."

"Well, I'm actually a computer systems guy," Ethan says. "Just doing this on the side. What about you?"

"Pest control. I'm a trapper."

"A trapper, exciting. Are you married, cohabitating?"

"I was married," Tyler says. "Like an idiot. Who gets married? Yeah, to Brooklyn Drummond—you remember her? We split up before we even unwrapped the gifts. Oh well, that was twenty years ago. Times were different. Before we figured out the Scandinavians were doin' it right. You?"

"Me? No. I've batted around the idea of doing the virtual dating thing."

"It's gotten way oversaturated, especially since the Bug."

The pod closes. Tyler rests his head on Ethan's chest. "Shall we?"

"This is pretty awkward, I gotta tell you," Ethan says.

"No, just do your thing. Pretend I'm a stranger."

Ethan puts his arms across the white robe covering Tyler's torso, rests his chin on top of his wiry nest. His head smells like a moist cavern.

"So why a male touch specialist?" Ethan says.

"Dude, I only go male now. I've been with plenty of ladies, nothing against them. I just prefer a firmer squeeze to take the edge off."

"Your best memory," Sandy says. "The best you've felt. The feeling you wish you could bottle."

"I have two," Ethan says, sipping on an Arnold Palmer from his living room sofa. The Moodselector kicks on, lights dim, wall color morphs from a dusty pink to a grey-blue. "Me and my dad, October 7, 2011, my first Brewers game. It's game five of the playoffs versus the Diamondbacks. Dad sold Mom's wedding ring for the tickets. I'm seven years old. There are forty thousand people in the stadium watching Nyjer Morgan, aka Tony Plush, step up to the plate in the bottom of the tenth. He hits a walk-off single to send the Brewers to the NLCS. We're showered with blue and gold confetti and Coors Light. There are fireworks erupting, people jumping up and down. I'll never see my dad so happy again, so comfortable with strangers. Years later, I realize he was quite intoxicated. Now I can't even remember the last time I went to the ballpark."

Sandy nods, hands clasped in her lap. "Mmm hmm." Katy Perry's oldie, "California Gurls," hums in the background.

"Second one," Ethan says, "me and Claire, December 27, 2032, The Big Island, Hawaii. Before the Bug. We're on a private tour with a man named Manuku. He takes us on a jungle hike and then leaves us under a secret waterfall where we quietly agree to make love, but then I'm too worried Manuku is watching us from behind a fern. Like a fool, I push her hand away when she puts it down my swim trunks. 'Claire!' I tell her. Other than Manuku, we don't see a single person on our hike the rest of the day. We drink water from fresh coconuts. We ride horses. We ultimately do make love in a crystal blue swimming hole, her red hair like a raging fire that can't be put out."

Ethan and Tyler are in the pod, embracing one another. It's dimly lit, illuminated only by the glow of time elapsing, and it smells like a decaying carcass. Wind chimes jingle in a summer evening breeze.

"I was thinking," Ethan says. He's nervous, like it's 2025 and he's asking a girl out for the first time. As he looks into Tyler's eyes—gray mainly but with hints of yellow and brown he's never noticed before—he realizes there is no one left on the planet he has known longer. "How about we move in together, become roomies, save on water?"

Tyler stares at him, grips his shoulders. His chapped lips part revealing marbled teeth. "Dude, that would be so Olympus Mons. I'm totally in."

Ethan scales back to one session with Sandy every other week. He goes to the dentist for a cleaning and has four cavities filled. The dental hygienist is a redhead who has a soft voice and smiles whenever she talks. She's not Claire, but she could be Claire 2.0.

Ethan squeezes on his old Brewers hat, stretches out his glove. He's bought two tickets, Brewers versus Cardinals. Tyler is happy to join him, and as soon as he comes home from lassoing an opossum, they head to the ball park together and sit behind the dugout under a giant red blister of a sun. The concrete under their shoes breathes generations of nacho cheese, Coca-Cola, and pretzel salt. Ethan sucks in the earth. It's honey down his throat.

Miller Park is crumbling. There are five thousand fans, and Ethan and Tyler could have a conversation from opposite sides of the diamond, but Ethan imagines the roar of forty thousand strong. When the Brewers load the bases, he and Tyler chest bump and high five. They put their arms over each other's shoulders, sing cheers in unison, and pound ice cold beers. There's the crack of the bat that reverberates through the stadium, and it's like a tropical birdsong in the heart of the Amazon.

THE UNCOUNTED

I had planned to stay in bed all day and into the night, miss the parades and fireworks and flag-lined streets, but Roger asked if I wanted to pack up and get away for the long weekend instead, across the border to a cheap beach resort in Mazatlán, where I wouldn't have to worry about anyone celebrating the Fourth of July, and I thought it would be a good idea.

I sat at the edge of the bed with barely enough energy to hold myself up, and sipped on a glass of warm water. It was 4:30 A.M., but I couldn't sleep. My stomach gnawed as if there were two hands reaching in and wringing it like a wet towel. I hadn't eaten in days. Didn't believe I deserved to. I imagined my body consuming itself to survive. Muscle and fat disappearing under the skin, from my cheeks, waist, breasts, ass.

Through the bedroom door, I peered into the living room at the memorial for Jeremy on the glass coffee table. His portrait shot was the centerpiece, in his dress blues, his hair clipped to the scalp, the hat much too big for his still-so-young head. The American flag was draped behind him. Of course he wasn't smiling because he wasn't supposed to. It seemed fitting. The Marine Corp quilt was thrown over the couch with the official emblem—Eagle, Globe, and Anchor—and an upside-down image of the two of us at his boot camp graduation. It was one of his proudest days. As the holiday weekend approached, I couldn't get rid of the thought, asleep or awake, that a mother's job was to protect her child.

My suitcase was packed and waiting by the front door. Roger would be there in a couple hours, but all I wanted to do was take the razor blade from my nightstand and carve up the inside of my thighs. Make the pain go away for even a minute. One of my rituals. When Jeremy first got deployed it resurrected all my worst vices. Cutting. Vomiting. Hand-washing until my skin went raw. They say it's about control when everything else is out of control. I had been through it when his dad, my ex-husband, had fought in Somalia, and Jeremy was just a baby. I knew the unwritten code. Be strong. Don't complain. Never distract your warrior when he's on deployment.

Roger hadn't seen my naked body yet in the light; we'd only had sex a handful of times and it was always in the dark. We would be on the beach though—couldn't avoid it. I thought about where I could cut myself without him seeing, without him asking questions. I forced myself up, opened a dresser drawer, and dug through some clothes until I found a dark purple sarong. I'd wear that. He wouldn't suspect a thing. Done. I walked to the front door, unzipped the suitcase, folded it nicely, rested it atop my neatly arranged clothes. I walked back into the bedroom, tore open an alcohol pad, and wiped my razor clean. My shorts slid down my bony legs.

Roger and I headed south down I-15 toward McCarran Airport. He let me drive. Traffic and weather droned on the radio. The windows were cracked open—the wind whipped around the cabin, did what it wanted with my hair—so I closed them. We passed the Strip. A few hours later, the temp would break a hundred and the streets would be swarming with tourists and locals. Hotel casinos, pools, and bars would be awash in patriotism. After the sun dropped, there would be concerts and fireworks. Of course, fireworks. Caesars Palace and Stratosphere would compete to put on the most impressive displays.

"Are you doing okay?" Roger asked.

"I don't know how I'm doing. Don't think okay is the right word. I'm here, I guess. Glad to be getting away."

"Well I'm glad we're doing this too. We'll have fun. It'll be good."

I stared out the window and watched the car devour the white lane markings. "Every year, Jeremy and I would go to the parade in Summerlin." I had been invited to this year's celebration to stand beside other military families and salute the veterans. To stand beside Uncle Sam on stilts. I politely declined. It was the first Fourth of July without Jeremy alive, without him somewhere on the planet, even if it had to be Kandahar.

Roger nodded and listened. I laughed. Didn't know why. "We'd eat pancakes and sing 'The Star-Spangled Banner,'" I said. "We'd wave our sparklers and watch the marching bands and floats and Macy's-style balloons glide by like ghosts."

When he was a kid, Jeremy would get all hot and sweaty in the bounce house and talk me into buying him a snow cone to cool off. The American flags painted on his face would be melting off. Those were the little stories that stayed between the two of us, went to the grave with us.

Planes took off and descended up ahead. I veered off the freeway at Sunset Road. Roger and I didn't know each other. Not really, not well. We started spending time together a few months after Jeremy's passing. Roger knew I had a son. Knew he was a Marine. Knew he was dead. But I never told him how he died. I think he assumed it was in combat, and why wouldn't he think that? Of course he would think that. We didn't talk much about things of substance which was fine by me. I liked having someone in the space beside me, but was turned off by much more than that. Roger seemed to feel the same way, though I didn't know what his story was. We met because my company was hired to clean his apartment once a week. I had cleaned it a few times myself. He invited me out to dinner one night, and I had nothing else to do. He seemed lonely. All I knew was he was a business consultant. He spent half his week in California where he worked. I presumed he secretly had a family there, a more exciting life. Or maybe he hated it and the desert was his escape. I never asked, he never told me.

We parked in the garage. He took the suitcases out of the trunk and pulled them along, the wheels rattling along the pavement. The brim of a straw safari hat fell over his eyes. Sunglasses hung from his neck by a strap.

"*Vamanos*," he said. "We don't want to miss our flight."

"Okay, okay." My lips cracked when I opened them. My poor heart could barely keep up with him.

Travelers hustled through the airport, rolling suitcases under palm trees, click-clacking across the tile floor. That morning, it was the busiest in the country. People lined the gold-plated slot machines, under a mural of old Las Vegas. Under Wayne Newton, the Stardust Casino, and Siegfried & Roy. You could hear the whir of spinning wheels, the beeps and chimes and clinking of coins dropping into metal pans. Cherries, lemons, number sevens.

"Do you gamble?" Roger asked, like he wanted to stop and try his luck.

"No. I hate it. Don't like flying either, for much the same reason."

We kept marching toward the gate and came up to a Starbucks.

"How about a coffee? I'm going to get one."

I shook my head. "No thanks."

I sat on a bar stool and waited for him. When military men and women passed, travelers saluted them. Thanked them for their service. I could see into the hollows of their eyes though, brothers in arms being blown to bits, losing limbs and lives, the Deployment Monster lurking, locked away in the deepest parts of their brains, reaching out and suffocating them unsuspectingly while they slept.

When we got to the gate, the sign said our flight had been delayed. Boarding time was pushed back three hours. Passengers groaned. They abandoned bags on vinyl seats, lined up to ask the gate attendant what was going on. I overheard someone say it was weather-related. Heavy rain along Mexico's Pacific coast. It was hurricane season.

"Ain't that a bitch," Roger said. He pulled a book out from his laptop case.

"I'm going to use the ladies room. Powder my nose."

After all that, I was going to be stuck in this country. In an airport of all places. Like it was a big joke. In a stall, I sat on the plastic seat cover and searched my purse for something to cut myself with. I had put a razor blade in my suitcase which didn't do me a damn bit of good then. There was nothing in my purse. I had a check book. I could cut a check. Give myself a paper cut. I laughed, then started crying, and threw the purse down onto the floor. I was tired and weak. The contents spilled under the stall door. A box of matches, tissues, and breath mints fell at women's feet as they washed their hands.

"Are you all right in there?" someone asked.

"I'm fine. Everything's fine in here. Go on."

As I walked back toward the gate, I heard a woman call my name. I turned. It took me a second to place her. We'd spent a lot of time together, way back when, but I couldn't remember her name for the life of me.

"Wendy McClaney," she said. "From the Bruner Elementary days."

"Yes, Wendy, wow."

"It's been a long time. How are you? I almost didn't recognize you. You've gotten so slim."

"That's what the Marines will do to you."

Wendy and I had been PTA moms years ago, during better days. We organized bake sales, books fairs, and family picnics. Our sons grew up together. They were on the same Boy Scout troop and Little League teams.

"We heard about Jeremy," she said. "I'm so sorry. And after everything he'd been through, I can only imagine you thought he was finally home safe."

"Yeah, the last couple years have been a rough go." I changed subjects. "How about you? Where are you headed?"

"We're going to see Patrick. He graduated from college. He lives in Boston now."

I needed to walk away. "Well tell everyone I say hello. Have a nice trip. It was good to see you, Wendy."

She reached in and gave me a hug. I didn't expect it. I could feel her hand rub the sharp edges of my shoulder blade. I didn't want her to let go.

"Take care of yourself," she said.

I started walking back to the gate, but felt hot and dizzy. The planes parked outside looked like they were moving. There were others in the sky I could swear were speeding toward the ground. Roger was lost in his book. He glanced up when I approached, then went back to it.

"I don't feel well," I said. Out of nowhere I had the thought that our plane was going to crash that day. It was going to be attacked. Jeremy was making me sick, warning me to run away and keep myself alive.

"Let me get you something to drink," Roger said.

"No, don't go. Please."

My head was throbbing and felt heavy like my neck couldn't hold it up much longer. I was lightheaded. I grabbed the rails of the seat. "Don't get on the plane," I said. My vision narrowed until I started slipping out of the seat, and there was nothing I could do to stop it. Everything went black.

I ended up in a hospital bed at the airport's Urgent Care Center. There was an IV plucked into the vein on the back of my hand. The tape had dry blood on it. A bag of fluid dripped overhead. Roger sat beside me.

"What did you tell your wife about this weekend?" I said. "Where does she think you are?"

"I don't have a wife. You know that, c'mon."

"Well why don't you? What's wrong with you?"

"My wife died ten years ago."

I sighed and put my hand on top of his. "I apologize, Roger. I'm a big jerk."

Roger took me back home. We sat in the living room, me in my pajamas curled up in the corner of the couch. The Marine quilt lay over my knees. The "Gold Star Family" flag hung in the window. We could hear the fireworks shows begin.

"Damn fireworks," Roger said. "Should we turn the TV up?"

"No, I want to see them."

We went outside and sat on the front steps. I sipped on chamomile tea. Roger drank a Dos Equis. He picked up a six-pack at the gas station on the way home. Said it was probably the closest he'd get to Mazatlán that year.

Up above, we watched fireworks burst. I had always loved them. The smell of gunpowder. The whistles and crackles and fizzles. Colored smoke. Falling stars. The illusion that the streaks of light were coming for you, getting bigger, before dying out. The grand finales.

"Do you want to know about Jeremy?" I said.

"Yeah, of course I do."

"I wish you could have met him. He was a wonderful kid. He wanted to be a Marine ever since he was six years old, just like his father. He enlisted when he was seventeen."

Mosquitos bit our ankles and wrists. I lit a citronella candle.

"He was twenty-three years old when he died. He'd done three year-long tours in Afghanistan."

"More than his share."

"When he came back from his last trip, he had PTSD in a bad way. He was drinking all the time. He rarely left the house. He was afraid of the dark. Once we were driving, and a train sounded its horn. He got so scared he jumped out of the car. After that, he never drove more than a few blocks."

"My God."

"He watched friends die and could never get over the fact that he didn't save them. He told me, 'You would hate me if you knew what I'd done out there.' I said, 'I could never hate you. You're my son.' He told me, 'No, Mom. The son you knew died over there.'"

There was nothing worse than for a mother to know her baby had gone to hell and back, and she'd done nothing to stop it. To protect him. That was what the men in their family did. And the women knew it, but didn't say anything. She knew it. *Never distract your warrior.*

"Jeremy killed himself," I said.

"I'm so sorry. I thought it might have been something like that."

"He shot himself in his bedroom closet. That's where he'd started sleeping at night, in his USMC sleeping bag."

I cried, and Roger put his arm around me. It had been nine months. From what I had read, life would never be easy for me again. The first year was supposed to be the hardest though. First Christmas without him, first birthday, first Fourth of July. It felt good to say his name out loud. To me, that was freedom. Telling his story I'd kept locked away for so long.

I wondered how many more women there were out there like me, hidden in dark rooms, pillows pulled down over heads, the booming of fireworks like aerial strikes.

Did world leaders consider us before declaring wars or were we the forgotten ones, the uncounted?

The fireworks finale began. Roger put his arm around my waist and pressed his hand against the cuts on my hip. It was like he knew. Like he was saying, *I'm not going to let you hurt yourself like that anymore. Not on my watch.* I wanted him to keep his hand right there, stop me from doing anything stupid, so I put my hand on top of his. Fireworks exploded over us in rapid succession. Brilliant whites and greens and blues. Lighting up the sky for a moment or two. And then they were done, just like that, only gray plumes of smoke left behind, and we could hear applause somewhere in the distance.

SIXTEEN HUNDRED CLOSEST FRIENDS

I friended Billy Dallas on Facebook. He accepted. To think it'd taken me this long to join the social media revolution.

"I can't believe you're not on Facebook?" my younger brother had said. Had taunted me. "Everybody's on Facebook."

I got harassed about it by one of the girls who worked for me at the diner too. Then the dental assistant when I went in for a routine cleaning, before finally giving in. My first friend request was less than twenty-four hours after launching my account—Raj, an Indian dude from my tenth grade Physics class I hadn't seen since 1992. I found Billy, my old childhood pal, a few days later.

My profile picture, carefully narrowed down from several possible choices, was of me and my wife, Irene. A selfie on our honeymoon, faces pressed against one another, the Mediterranean Sea behind us. "Who's the chick, bro?" Billy commented on my wall. Must've not bothered to look at my relationship status.

I spent an hour and a half sitting in front of the desktop in our basement, navigating through Billy's page. It'd been about four years since I'd last spied on him via MySpace. I wondered periodically if his vast social network had come crumbling down with the demise of the site. Maybe I secretly hoped it had. But, he'd clearly come back bigger than before—1,617 Facebook friends. From a dozen Angies to a handful of Zoes. I'd never even come across one Zoe in my entire life. The guy had always been popular, but goddamn.

"Sam, what are you doing?" Irene called from the living room. She was watching *Dancing with the Stars*. She knew it wasn't like me to miss it.

"Paying online bills, baby," I said.

Billy's profile pic was the expected: linen shirt unbuttoned past his chest, skin Miami-tanned, teeth white as a wedding dress. He looked like he was still twenty-five. His interests: traveling the globe to listen to the best live DJ sets, beach volleyball, reading a good book. The Billy I knew couldn't even get through an audio book.

A post from a girl who went by the name Karolina Poland popped up on his wall: "Hey cutie. Sound-Bar tonight?"

It was a Tuesday.

Unlike some people, I was up at four A.M. the next day. Shit, I was up at four every day. I'd hit the snooze button twice, be at the diner by five. Never liked getting up that early, but it hadn't ever really bothered me as much as it did that morning. I wondered if Billy and Karolina Poland had even gotten home yet from the night before. Or maybe they were naked, rolling around under his silk bed sheets while I was opening shop and getting the coffee pots brewing. I really needed to get the Internet hooked up there.

Dan, a retired electrician, came in at 5:45 with the *Sun Times* tucked under his arm, just like he did every day. Diner Dan. He sat at the counter, his back hunched, sipping on his usual cup of black coffee.

"What's on tap this week?" he said. "Any big plans?"

"Just hanging out with the wife. Same thing I always do."

"You're still young. You should be living it up, married or not. When I was your age, I was out every night. Everyone in this city knew me—every bar owner, cocktail waitress, bookie."

Dan used to meet up at the diner with his buddies. They'd guzzle down pots of coffee, devour skirt steaks (all the way down to the fat), and go through packs of Marlboro Reds. But one by one, his friends started dropping off. Paul the Painter was serving three years for tax evasion; Gus, the long-time maître d' at a swanky downtown restaurant, stopped coming around after his wife caught him with an Asian masseuse; Vegas, who made his living at the track, had disappeared two years earlier between March Madness and the Kentucky Derby.

I slid Dan a piece of pumpkin pie. It matched his dyed hair. "I'm here twelve hours a day," I said. "Been working since I was thirteen, you know that. Never had the time to chase around cocktail waitresses like you."

"Wait 'til you have kids. Then, you can really forget about it."

For the last month, Irene and I had been in talks about when we'd start "trying." By trying, she meant visiting the doc for pre-conception planning, keeping track of her menstrual cycle on the kitchen calendar, graphing her basal body temperature, and stuffing a pillow under her rear while we made love so my boys could make it to their destination. She wasn't messing around.

"Kids," Diner Dan said. "Now that's a game-changer."

For most of the day, I sat in the booth closest to the register, getting up to ring out customers or shoot the shit with my cop and firefighter regulars. I downed five cups of java by day's end. Talked to Irene about ten times, figured out what we were going to have for dinner, what we'd watch on the tube. By late afternoon, I wondered if Billy and Karolina Poland had even started the day yet. Maybe they were in the shower, Karolina's hands leaving prints on the steamy glass, Billy behind her giving neck kisses, while I was at the bank on the way home, making the day's deposit.

Every night that week I ended up in the basement spying on Billy. I couldn't help myself. On top of that, I was amassing new friends every day. People I barely even knew—dudes I met at the gym, customers from the diner, my dry cleaner. I was already almost at twenty-five.

"What are you doing down there?" Irene would say.

"Checking e-mail, sweetie."

I swear, within the week, Billy's relationship status had changed from "single" to "in a relationship" back to "single" again. It took me days to get through his photos—all 968 of them. *The guy's a loser*, I said to myself. *He doesn't want to ever grow up.* I kept clicking through his pics. *These girls he's with look like teenagers, the predator!* I kept clicking. I scanned through his friends again. My nineteen-year-old busboy, Eduardo, was even on his list. Eduardo, for Chrissake! Was there anyone in this city Billy didn't know?

One night Irene snuck up on me before I could click back to the ESPN homepage. On the screen was a picture of Billy, sun-kissed, waist-deep in the Atlantic Ocean, an open coconut in his hands. Pretty sure he was flexing his abs. I muttered the caption to myself: "Fresh coconut anyone?"

"Who the hell is that?" Irene said, like she'd just busted me searching gay porn.

"Just some guy I used to know, honey."

She sat down next to me in her pajama pants and baggy T-shirt, glasses on. She browsed his latest postings: Billy Dallas "just ate twelve hard-boiled egg whites and is about to hit the gym, baby!" at 7:05 P.M.; Billy Dallas "has sore fucking abs" by 8:15.

"Our dads were from the same village in Greece," I explained. "We lived right down the street from each other so, you know, the old men would get together to play backgammon and bullshit. Billy and I would play videogames and street football, breakdance. We were practically best friends until junior high."

"Wait, you used to breakdance?"

"Yeah, I was a b-boy for about a year in '84."

I didn't have the balls to tell my own wife by the time Billy and I were in high school, he wanted to have no part anymore in videogames or street football or breakdancing. Or me. He was going to parties experimenting with booze and sex while I was having sleepovers on weekends with the only two close buddies I had.

Before long, Irene and I were clicking through Billy's pictures together, following him on his adventures from Mykonos to Ibiza to London to Tokyo. Two voyeurs. We read the comments below each pic from his circle of female admirers: "Amazing," "Holy abs. Yummy!", "Oooh don't you look GQ?", "Nerd. Jk. (kinda)."

"Did you used to be like this?" Irene asked.

"No, of course not, baby." I wished. "We grew apart in high school. I've barely seen him since. I started working with my dad at the diner, I was busy all the time. You know how it goes."

"I can't believe you were ever friends with this guy."

"Well, he kind of changed after puberty. He was actually a pretty nice kid."

In the time it took us to go through Billy's pics, he'd added four new friends. Irene eventually got bored and went upstairs to do the dishes. I told her I'd be right there. I stared at a photo of Billy in some random packed club, God knows where on the map. His arms were wrapped around two bleach blondes damn near half our age, all three with shots in hand. His face looked swollen from the sun. The girls' eyes were half shut, hair wild, tits spilling out of their tops. He'd probably ended up working his way through an assortment of kama sutra positions with both of them that night. I was disgusted and envious at the same time. Irene's tits were the only two I'd ever see again and they'd be shriveled to nothing after six months of breastfeeding, from what I'd heard.

"*American Idol* is starting, Sam!" Irene called. "Hurry up!"

Irene left a few days later to visit her sister in Philly who'd just popped out her second kid. Field training in swaddling, burping, and diaper changing. I had to stay back and keep an eye on the diner.

"You won't even miss me," she said. "You've been so glued to that Facebook lately."

It took me a second (I was updating my list of favorite movies), but I shut off the monitor and stood up. "Of course I'm gonna miss you." I leaned in to kiss Irene's forehead and smudged her glasses.

"When I get back, I guess we'll start trying ourselves, huh?" she said.

I nodded. "Will do, honey."

I drove Irene to O'Hare. She wheeled the suitcase behind her. I waved as she passed the security checkpoint. When I got home, the house was dark and quiet. We hadn't spent a night apart since the day before our wedding. I turned on the TV, but it wasn't the same watching *The Bachelorette* without her. I shut it off, walked down the creaky steps to the basement, and sat down at the computer.

Irene made it into Philly. I stayed up past my usual bedtime, spying. Voyeurism wasn't quite as much fun alone, though, either. I scrolled down Billy's wall: "Crobar tomorrow night with DJ Inphinity! Email me if you want to be on the guest list."

I found some old pictures on my computer from a bachelor party in Vegas Billy and I had both ended up at six years earlier. Some guy who'd grown up with us down the block. It was the last time I'd actually seen Billy. I decided to post one of them. Called it "Back in the Day." It was a shot of me, Billy, the groom (since divorced), and a few other dudes. We were standing in front of a line of showgirls, our arms across each other's shoulders. I had a cigarette tucked behind my ear even though I didn't smoke. By the end of the night, four people had commented they liked the pic, flashing the "thumbs up" symbol.

On a whim, I decided to IM Billy. I wrote: What's up? The wife's out of town. Why don't you swing by the old neighborhood for a BBQ before you go out tomorrow night?

He responded, to my surprise.

Billy Dallas: Cool. You can roll out with me to the club afterward.

Sam Nikas: Wish I could, but gotta be up at four.

Billy Dallas: Come on, your woman's out of town. She'll probably be out dancing at the club herself.

Sam Nikas: Her sister just had a—

Billy Dallas: When was the last time you partied, dog? You should take advantage of the freedom. Return of the mack.

I loved that song.

The next morning, I woke up before the alarm even sounded and got into the diner early. I had the coffee brewing and the machines running before the employees got in. I watered all the plants. I even started shredding the hashbrown potatoes myself. Diner Dan came in at 5:45.

"How ya' doing, Dan-o?" I said. I poured him a cup of coffee. Decided to let him have it on the house.

"What's on tap this weekend?" he asked.

"I'm heading downtown with a friend tonight. One of my boys. Should be fun."

"Good for you. About time. You should stop by the Como Inn. That was one of my old stomping grounds. Tell 'em Dan sent you." I didn't have the heart to tell him the place had been torn down a decade earlier to put up townhouses.

When I was done working, I ran to get a haircut. Then I stopped by the mall to find something cool to wear. I'd torn through my closet the night before and come up with nothing. I popped my head into stores I'd never even heard of—H&M, Urban Outfitters, Forever 21 (which apparently was for girls only)—before finally finding a shirt with images of skulls and wings and lightning that looked like something out of Billy's photos. I swung by the grocery store and picked up a case of Bud Light and a pack of stogies.

By the time Billy made it over, forty-five minutes late, I had brats sizzling on the grill and Armin Van Buuren playing in the background (the 2003 album—most recent one I could dig up).

From the backyard, I heard his Harley roaring down our quiet suburban street. I happened to glance over at our garden tucked away in the corner of the yard. I remembered when Irene and I went to Home Depot to pick out our plants. There were so many choices: San Marzano tomatoes, beefsteak tomatoes, cherry tomatoes. "Isn't this so much fun?" she'd said. It was, but now I couldn't help but envision myself earlier in the summer, on hands and knees, planting lettuce while Billy was probably just leaving some club after last call.

I cut through the house, tongs in hand, and eyed Billy through the screen door. He was in a tank top, sleeve tattoos covering both arms, empty-handed with the exception of an open can of Red Bull.

"Yo, yo, where've you been, dog?" Billy said. He clasped my hand and gave me a back-slap. His hair, brushed up and molded into place with firm-hold gel, scratched my cheek as he reached in.

"I've been around," I said. I lived three-quarters of a mile from my childhood home. I gave Billy a good once-over from close range. He looked different than I'd expected from his Facebook pics. His face was leaner; wrinkles radiated from the corners of his eyes down to the corners of his mouth. I was relieved not to be the only one with a receding hairline. "You don't age," I lied. "When I saw your pictures on Facebook, I thought you'd discovered the Fountain of Youth."

"Awe, I Photoshop all those pics. That's just my brand."

I grabbed a couple beers from the fridge, and we moved to the backyard. Billy sat at the patio table, while I stood at the grill dodging smoke.

"I forgot how quiet it was out here in the country," he said.

"We're only like twenty minutes from downtown."

"Maybe it's just 'cause the city's always poppin'," Billy said. "I have an apartment in the Gold Coast. It feels like we're in the middle of Wisconsin right now." He took a swig of beer. I noticed him take a long look at the garden from behind his Versace shades.

"So, what's been going on with you?" I said. I turned the brats. The juices dripped onto the coals, aggravating the flames. "I haven't seen you in years. Since Vegas, I think."

It took him a second. "Oh yeah, Vegas. The bachelor party. I forgot you went with us. That was off the chain. I slept with that Cirque du Soleil dancer." He looked off into the distance like he was trying to evoke images of the encounter. "Anyway, I was bouncing at a club for a while, now I'm kinda managing it. I'm still out every night, traveling like crazy. My friends just keep getting younger, that's all that changes."

I took a couple brats off the grill and dropped them into buns.

"So your dad's produce store—you guys got rid of it, right?" I said. My dad had already told me the land had been sold to Costco when Billy refused to take over the business.

"Couldn't do it, my man," Billy said. "I might as well have been in the clink. Waking up before sunrise, surrounded by the same four walls, smelling fruit all day, every day. I'd be bored as hell. I'd go crazy."

There was silence. Crickets chirping.

"You? What do you do?" he asked.

"Me?" I could feel my face turning red, like the big boy tomatoes hanging in the garden. "Just at the diner still. Yeah, I run it now, so…"

"No shit?" Billy said. "Good for you, buddy. Good for you. Took the plunge. Own the diner. Nice and settled. Good for you."

After dinner, we walked around the yard, examining the garden, smoking stogies. Billy pulled his iPhone from his pocket and looked at it. "We should head out," he said. "You ready?"

I was on my third beer. "Definitely," I said.

Billy had insisted on driving. "You ain't gonna find a spot to park your mini-van downtown, dog," he said.

Irene would kill me if she found out I'd been on the back of a motorcycle going ninety on the Kennedy. We stopped by Billy's place, a seven-hundred-square-foot junior one-bedroom on the twentieth floor, with floor-to-ceiling windows and a sprawling view of Lake Michigan. He had a monster canister of whey protein on the granite counter and some furniture arranged around a 52-inch flat screen TV. Above his black leather sofa was a life-size portrait of himself smoking a cigarette on a beach.

"Cool painting," I said.

"This Spanish chick I hooked up with in Majorca gave it to me." It was based on a picture she'd taken of him just after they'd made love in the sand, he said.

I peeked into Billy's closet while he showered. He had two dozen belts with various buckles hanging from the back of the door. There was a Native American Indian buckle, a bald eagle, a Texas longhorn. Crazy how different our lives had become. His biggest concern was probably which one he was going to wear to the club that night; mine was when exactly my wife would be ovulating. He chose the eagle.

We sped down the elevator packed in with five other people, no one saying a word. I was excited. A little nervous too. I told Irene I was going to see a movie. I thought it'd be best.

When we got to the club, there was a line out the door. Billy knew the doorman, though, so we didn't even pay. He pushed his way through the crowd towards the VIP section. I tried not to lose him. Bodies pressed against one another; hands reached up to avoid spilling cocktails.

"It's my friend's birthday," Billy yelled over the blaring music. He gave the VIP attendant a kiss on the cheek and a little small talk, and the velvet rope was lifted.

A group of people stood up from a small table as we walked in. There was a bottle of vodka chilling in a bucket of ice and carafes of cranberry juice and OJ. I recognized faces from Billy's list of friends. There was a lanky dude who went by the screen name Muscles. There was an emaciated blonde with 600cc in her chest and orange skin.

"Is that Karolina Poland?" I leaned in and asked him.

"Karolina who? Oh, no. I kicked that chick to the curb."

I stood behind Billy while he chatted. He tried to introduce me, but I could tell he didn't know all their names.

"This is one of my dogs," he told the birthday girl. I swear she must've been turning eighteen.

We sat down at the table. They talked about DJs, who was hooking up with whom, what clubs were hot that night. We took shots together. Jägerbombs, Kamikazes, Red-headed Sluts. I got tipsy for the first time since a wedding Irene and I had been to the summer before. We fist-pumped, me and my new friends.

"Are you on Facebook?" someone asked me.

Of course I was. I was one of Billy's sixteen hundred closest friends.

The girls all jumped up when a Lady Gaga remix started pounding over the speakers. Billy and Muscles followed them onto the dance floor.

"I'll meet you out there," I said.

It was already after midnight. I had a headache and could barely keep my eyes open. I stood at the bar sipping on a gin & tonic. Billy posed for pictures with the birthday girl, lips pursed, chest flexed. Those pics would make their way onto Facebook, no doubt. I bummed a cigarette from some kid and almost lit the wrong end. At about 12:30, Irene sent me a text. "Going to bed," she said. "Love ya." I started to text her back when I felt a hand on my shoulder.

"Mr. Nikas?"

I turned around. It was Eduardo, my busboy.

"Man, didn't expect to see you here, boss!" he said.

Billy approached and ordered another round of shots from the bar. His face was sweaty, the bags under his eyes more pronounced. He bobbed his head to the music and stared at the bartender's cleavage.

I leaned in and yelled into Eduardo's ear. "Actually, I'm here with an old friend. I think you guys know each other. I saw you're one of his Facebook friends." I turned to Billy. "Hey, don't you know my guy over here—Eduardo? He works for me."

Maybe I should have been embarrassed to be seen there—tied for oldest guy in the club and likely the only one referred to as "Mr." that night. Or maybe I'd have a newfound respect from Eduardo that would trickle down to the rest of the busboys, the cooks, the waitresses. I wouldn't just be the boring married dude with the five o'clock shadow who sat around drinking coffee and barking out orders all day.

Billy gave Eduardo the once-over. He shook his head. "No, I don't think we've ever met." He extended his hand. "Nice to meet you, dog."

Eduardo slid off into the crowd. Billy and his crew downed another round of Jägerbombs. I went to take a piss and bumped into some girl who spilled her green apple martini all over my brand new designer T-shirt. As I swayed across the urinal, I stared at the picture on my cell phone of me and Irene at a corn maze, mid-October 2008. I texted her goodnight.

Billy stood looking at me, hands on his hips. "You really gotta go? DJ Inphinity, man! You can crash at my crib. I've got two Cubs tickets for tomorrow."

"Yeah," I said, "I have to open the diner at five, and I'm picking up Irene in the afternoon."

He clasped my hand and wrapped his arm around my back. "That sucks, my man. Oh well, we'll do it again, right?" His eyes darted through the club; his hand stayed rested on my shoulder. "I still can't believe it—married, own the diner, pretty soon you'll have a house full of kids. Good for you, brother. Good for you." His breath smelled like Jäger. Before I left, he reminded me to check his Facebook page the next day for pictures from the night.

I hailed down a taxi and jumped in. When I told the cabbie I was headed to the burbs, he muttered something under his breath. Something about the "fuckin' country" and didn't speak for the rest of the ride. I called Irene's cell.

"Honey? What are you still doing up?" she said in a whisper.

"I'm actually just heading home."

"So late? How was the movie?"

"It was all right," I said. "Nothing like the previews."

Irene sent a picture of our new nephew to my phone. "I'm so excited to start a family with you. Our own little family."

I leaned my head back and kicked off my shoes. My feet were sore. My wet designer T-shirt clung to my chest. I secretly dreaded sleeping in our old two-story colonial by myself, the floors creaking all night long, the king bed big and empty without Irene spread out across the other half.

RED CLAY

When Gustavo asked her to meet him in Mexico for a "worry-free fuckfest," Meera said, "Yeah, sure," mostly because she never wanted to be the girl who said no to something she wasn't supposed to do. Now she's curbside at Benito Juárez Airport, suitcase safe against her leg, wondering how the hell she agreed to fly there alone and then ride three hours in a private taxi to "El Rancho," as he calls it—her, all of a hundred and five pounds, bones jetting at the hips like rocks from a path. This is crazy even by her standards. There's usually at least someone in her big Indian family trying to tag along, and now, here she stands, off the radar in a foreign land no less. She doesn't even speak a lick of Spanish.

Horns are honking. Pasty midwesterners climb on coach buses headed to Cuernavaca and Puebla. A giant bottle of Real Hacienda 100% Agave seems to be offering her a slug from a billboard across the street.

Gustavo sent her an awkward text message when the plane landed, welcoming her and saying he would see her shortly. The message is written in the way a boss is supposed to communicate with his employees, like their meeting is actually business related. Apparently the guy's got a conscience all of a sudden.

A black Lincoln Town Car with tinted windows pulls up beside her. The driver pops out—short, stocky, broad face, hooked nose. Minus the black suit, he's what she pictures the Aztecs looked like.

"Meera Atwal?" He has a sign with her name on it, except there are mistakenly two ls in Atwal. Gustavo doesn't even know how to spell her last name.

"That's me," she says.

"*Bienvenidos a México.* Welcome."

Meera, of course, lied to her parents, told them she was going on a business trip to Cancún. Important conference. The company was putting them up in the beachside Marriott. She was traveling with several coworkers—Jenny Flores, Pete Huffman, Deb Romano. She threw in an Indian girl too. Nishi Chandha. Nishi doesn't really exist, but her parents always seem more at ease when there's a fellow Indian in the mix.

"Whatever you do," her dad said, "don't drink the water."

The driver lifts Meera's suitcase and lays it in the trunk. She slides into the leather backseat hesitantly. Everything she's read about Mexico City warns never, ever to get into an unauthorized cab. The books say to look for the yellow cabs with plastic white TAXI signs lit up on the roofs and TRANSPORTACION TERRESTRE painted across the doors. There are countless stories of phony cabbies, robberies and beatings. As the car blends into traffic, Meera imagines a horrible hoax is being played on her, maybe even orchestrated by Gustavo himself, that she's going to be kidnapped and ransomed. Her parents will kill her when she's eventually set free and back home unless she's beheaded first like those poor victims of drug wars she sees on the news. There's a part of her, she realizes, that thinks that's what she deserves.

Meera was pretty sure she wasn't qualified for the position as Marketing Manager. She was green, straight out of college, up against many a seasoned candidate. She applied anyway. When Gustavo hired her, her family threw a big party because this was precisely the American Dream they'd sought. Not that Indians needed much of a reason to throw a party. Ain't no party like a Punjabi party. Tables overflowing with makki ki roti and sarson ka saag, the men all in one room talking shit, mom's brother's brother-in-law breaking out into Punjabi song. Now, as the car eats up long stretches of lush Mexican countryside, Meera realizes she definitely wasn't qualified for the position after all.

Gustavo isn't a good-looking man by any means, though he gives the impression he thinks he is. He's in his forties with the beady eyes of a hamster and acne scars, proof of mythical teenage battles on his cheeks. His frame is soft but imposing. He probably could have played football or basketball had he grown up in the States, had he bothered to lift weights, but he hadn't. In fact, even though he's from Mexico, he says he's never played soccer either. If anything, he's an armchair quarterback for his darling Cowboys.

Gustavo didn't wait long to begin his onslaught of grossly inappropriate behavior and feeble passes at her. On Meera's first day at work he said, "Man, do I love the breast," as he was passing through the cafeteria and saw her slicing through a piece of chicken. He referred to her exclusively as "sweetie" and "hon" especially in team meetings. Every Friday, he asked her where her boyfriend was taking her out, even though she'd made it clear there was no boyfriend. He made his pass at the holiday party between the punch bowl and seven layer nacho dip. He was staying overnight at the hotel and told her he had some important documents in his room he needed to show her. "It'll just take a minute," he said. He wasn't exaggerating by much. As he kissed the back of her neck under the buzz of the bathroom lights he whispered, "I'm down with the brown, baby," and still she had sex with him.

The driver has a picture of his family on the dashboard, like the one Gustavo has on his desk at work of his two little runts, his wife, all in cowboy hats or sombreros. Meera doesn't know the difference. In the picture, his wife comes across as a woman who likes to be in charge: big boobs, square shoulders, a sturdy ass, and yet apparently confident in tight jeans. Meera doesn't know her name, doesn't want to know it. But in her head, when she thinks of her, her name is Gustava.

"I have a cousin in Chicago," the Aztec says. "He works at a restaurant. Do you know Applebees?"

Meera puts her earbuds back in and cranks some Killer Mike. The Aztec will keep yapping otherwise, asking her questions about Michael Jordan, Al Capone, and deep dish pizza. She gazes out the window at the landscape. She never thought she'd see Mexico. She feels so far away from everything she knows. She thought she'd like that but now she's not so sure she does. They come to a small village with a church and a little plaza, palm trees and stray dogs.

"Let's stop here for a break," he says.

Meera steps out. A woman approaches with skin like hers—the color of red clay—and a baby strapped to her back by a cloth. Meera can only see the baby's red clay legs poking out. The woman tries selling her a wooden comb or tourist pen or knock-off Gucci watch.

"No speako Español," Meera says, but the woman doesn't give up. She's gesturing to her baby, Meera assumes saying something about how they're poor, how she needs to feed those clay legs, how she'll do anything for her baby including walking around all day selling useless trinkets at the risk of becoming a hunchback. Meera gives the woman ten American dollars in exchange for a Virgin of Guadalupe keychain.

She lights a cigarette and calls home. "Hey mom, how are you? Yeah, the flight was good. I sat next to Nishi. We talked about her sister's big Punjabi wedding the whole way here."

Meera wishes she could be honest, talk to her mom like American girls talk to their moms. She wishes she could tell her she's alone in the middle of nowhere, that she's sleeping with a married man who also happens to be her boss, that unbeknownst to her parents she's actually been impure for a long, long time. She wishes she could tell her mom all of this without the fear she'll be kicked out of the house, banished from the family forever. She blows cigarette smoke away from the phone because her mom has no idea she does that either.

There's a market in the plaza. They're selling everything from mangos to pet birds to pirated DVDs. Meera buys some gummy worms to snack on. A few weeks earlier, Gustavo had presented her with the Gumby Award at a staff meeting, for being the team's most flexible member.

In his office afterward, she stood with her arms folded, face warm, telling him she couldn't believe he'd done that. Gustavo snorted, tried patting her ass. She pushed his arm away and looked toward the door. "Relax," he said. "Nobody knows anything. I actually thought it was hilarious." She admired his boldness.

El Rancho is surrounded by rugged mountains. There are cows grazing in the distance, some horses beside the house. Meera rolls her suitcase to the door while dust rises. Her stomach is swirling. She rings the bell and sees an older woman approaching through the glass window. The woman is slow, fragile, wrinkles like canyons, hair like a gray wolf's. Meera assumes she's the housekeeper.

"*Buenas tardes*," the woman says and smiles.

"Um, I don't speak any Español."

"That's okay. I speak English."

"Oh, good. Well, I'm here to see Gustavo."

"Gustavo will be back shortly. Please come in. I am his mother."

Meera turns back, but the Aztec is already pulling away.

Inside, El Rancho is welcoming, sandy brown tiles and pale orange walls, sunlight streaming in from the windows. Gustavo's mother offers Meera a seat on the yellow couch. She brings her a glass of water. Meera hopes it's bottled because she well knows what kind of hell a person can pay for drinking from the Mexican tap. She looks around for

Gustavo. Part of her wants him to walk in right then and another part hopes he broke his neck riding on a horse. His mother sits beside her, hands in her lap.

"So tell me—how did you and Gustavo meet?"

"We met at work. I work for him actually. He's my boss."

Against her better judgment, Meera guzzles the water. She wishes it was tequila.

"Do you like your job?"

"I'm starting to think I might be in over my head."

"Well, I believe Gustavo has done well with the company. He's done well in America. He's provided for our family, his wife, my beautiful grandchildren. He built El Rancho." Her knees are practically touching Meera's now. "His only problem is he's become full of machismo, and that makes me sad. But, I cannot do anything about it. He's a grown man."

Meera places her water down and stands up. "May I use your bathroom, please?"

"Let me ask you something, Meera. Why did you come here?"

"Why?" Meera isn't sure how to respond to that. *Because I'm a grown woman*, she wants to declare. *Because I can do whatever the fuck I want with my life*, even though she knows that's not a great answer. "Gustavo invited me," she says instead.

152

"I know how my Gustavo is. He's invited many friends here before. But a young, pretty girl like you—I can't imagine what would bring you here."

"I have to use your bathroom now, ma'am."

Meera hurries off. She stares at herself in the bathroom mirror. Her eyes are dry and red. Looking out the window, she plans her escape. She wishes she could have her parents pick her up like a drunken teenager at a house party. Maybe she'll jump on one of the broncos and ride it back to the airport. Problem is, she doesn't know where the hell in Mexico she is exactly, and she doesn't have a map. Not her first mistake. She hears the door open and Spanish being spoken rapid-fire. It's Gustavo. She lights a cigarette and calls her mom.

"Hey, it's me again. I think I screwed up."

"What happened? Where are you?"

"I know you guys warned me not to, but I drank the water."

Gustavo knocks on the door. "Meera, are you in there?"

Meera covers the phone with her hand. She wishes she was on the plane heading back to Chicago. She imagines herself sitting next to Nishi, sharing her gummy worms, gabbing away about her sister's wild Punjabi wedding again.

"Meera?" he keeps saying. "Are you there? Is my Meera in there?"

KINGDOM COME

Pauly flicks a toothpick back and forth from one side of his mouth to the other, chews on it until he can feel splinters against his tongue. Ed, one of his regulars, wants to know if he's heard the news. The owner of Eighties restaurant across the street is going to be crowned Hot Dog King by the City of Detroit.

"Yeah, I heard something about that."

Ed wipes his hands on the back of his jeans, pushes up his glasses with an oily index finger, smudges a lens. "Your dad was the original Hot Dog King."

"Then the city turned into a ghost town, buddy boy. Whose fault is that?"

Pauly looks out at his kingdom of four empty tables. When he was a kid and his old man was running the joint, times were different. They had the Big Three automakers and lines out the door. Coney Island style hot dogs. Natural casing. Family secret chili sauce. Fresh-chopped white onions. A squeeze of yellow mustard.

Darryl, the cook, peeks out from the opening behind the register. A Tigers game is fuzzy on the mounted tube TV. The A/C window unit wheezes like an asthmatic.

Ed dumps his grease-soaked paper bag into the trash, and Pauly walks him out. The gray sky blends into the gray buildings. The city smells like cars burning. Pauly looks across Lafayette Street at Eighties.

"People don't go there for the food, my man," Pauly says. "He ropes 'em in with gimmicks. His Coney sauce is a soup. Do you know how many businesses I've watched come and go in that same spot?"

"I remember there being a Hardees for a while," Ed says. "A Cottage Inn Pizza…"

"Yessir, keep going. Don't forget the Jack in the Box."

The last incarnation before Eighties moved in a year earlier was a vacant lot. Urban wilderness. A burial ground for used tires, old furniture, and Bible-themed coloring books.

Tomorrow night the Eighties parking lot will be packed with 1980s muscle cars. Camaros, Trans Ams, Firebirds. Suburban families will be pulling up in minivans, kids will be piling out of sliding doors. Motor City Monday Nights. It'll be a seven-day extravaganza this week, the last of the summer. Through its windows, Pauly can make out the wall-to-wall posters of Robocop, Madonna, and Barry Sanders. There are cardboard cutouts of Transformers that kids can stick their mugs into for photo ops. Megatron. Dinobot. More than meets the eye.

"Does he even realize Barry Sanders played most of his career in the nineties?" Pauly says.

"The city is embracing him."

Pauly knows Detroit is looking for heroes. Hopes are hung on people ready to resuscitate it. America loves a comeback story.

"People are suckers, my man," Pauly says. "We've been here since the 1950s and, watch, we'll still be slugging it out when that chump's long gone."

A half-eaten hot dog rests in the wrapper in front of Pauly's nephew, Austin.

"Your dog's gonna get cold. They're made to be eaten right away."

"I'm good, Uncle Pauly."

"Is the bun stale? Darryl, open up a new bag of buns!"

Austin is his little brother's son. He just started his first semester at Wayne State University in Midtown, getting his Master's in Urban Planning. Pauly is letting him crash at his place until he finds an apartment. Austin's parents moved the family out to Minneapolis before the kids got to high school. Now Austin has come back to help be part of Detroit's renaissance. Detroit 2.0. He shops at Whole Foods, the only one in the city. Pauly finds it endearing.

"That's our family secret Coney sauce," Pauly says. "It's in your blood. You don't like it?"

"I like it, I like it."

"Then what's the problem?"

"I was just thinking. Have you ever thought about updating the restaurant?"

"So it can look all pristine like the place across the street? No thank you. This is a hot dog joint. We rely on good food, which I stand by. Why, what would you do differently?"

Austin runs his hand along the tears in the vinyl of the seats. He nods to the layer of dust on the blades of the ceiling fan. "Invest in some new chairs, brighten the place up. Definitely get a cleaning crew in here."

"Hey that's character, buddy boy. That represents years of hard work. You don't earn dust like that by burying your nose in textbooks." Pauly gets up to pace. His shoes stick to the floor. "Look, you worry about fixing Detroit and the people will flock back. Trust me. This city's always loved us."

Motor City Monday. Pauly and Darryl sit in folding chairs outside of the shop. Darryl lights a menthol cigarette.

"Let me bum one of those," Pauly says. He doesn't usually smoke. It ignites his lungs.

Across the street at Eighties, kids are being pushed in strollers. Dads wander from Mustangs to Impalas. Local camera crews circulate, take footage, interview families. Sloppily-made Coney dogs stain shirts. *You'd never know half of Detroit City was being bulldozed down as we speak,* Pauly thinks. The hulking remains of crumbling factories. Abandoned gas stations stripped down to rusty canopies and fuel dispensers. Homes without windows and doors. All that history being swept away—good, bad, and the ugly—because everybody wants to forget it existed. Because Detroit needs to forget it existed and start anew.

"When my dad handed this place over to me, I wanted to franchise it, take it nationwide," Pauly says.

"Why didn't you?"

Pauly doesn't respond because he doesn't have an answer. He watches the sign get hung anointing the owner of Eighties "Detroit's Hot Dog King." Another sign is being erected that says, "Home of the World Famous Coney Dog." He leans back against the cracked brick façade.

"We built this city with your pops," Darryl says. He hoots. "We had some big fun, didn't we?"

"I love Motown, slim."

Darryl is his dad's guy. He's been with them since the seventies. When Pauly was a kid, he'd let him help cut the potatoes into strips and dunk them into the deep fryer. There are a lot of memories there. He would sit in the booth for hours back then, gathering salt and pepper shakers, pretending they were soldiers at war. The regulars would greet him, tussle his hair. His dad would get free tickets and take him along to Red Wings and Lions games.

"Our reputation don't mean anything no more," Pauly says. He stubs the cigarette in the pavement and looks Darryl in the eyes, grabs his arm and squeezes it like they're both pepper shakers in a losing battle.

"I'm doing my best, boss man," Darryl says. "The kitchen's tore up from the floor up. I can't go on cooking like that."

"I'm gonna be honest, the IRS is on my ass. I'm six months behind on sales taxes. They can shut us down any day. I haven't told anybody."

"Shoot. And I haven't got paid in three weeks."

"Give me another couple days."

Pauly can't remember the last time he wore a monkey suit. His brother's wedding? He's wearing one now. The top button won't reach the hole. The suit jacket tugs at his back. He flips through the menu while he sits at the bar and waits for the owner. This is one of the city's new hot spots. Voted the best place in Detroit for a craft cocktail, whatever that is exactly. They serve organic wine. The bartender is in a vest and tie. The walls are covered with Midwest taxidermy. White-tailed deer. Pheasant. Barred owls.

The owner comes back out. "Sorry about that. So you were saying?" He wears a fancy silver watch. His eyes dart around the bar.

"I was just saying, I've been in the restaurant business since I was knee-high. I've managed our family-run place for the last eleven years. I'm just looking for something different. Something fresh."

"Any experience managing a bar?"

"No. I considered getting a liquor license at our restaurant, but no. I've been to quite a few bars, though."

The owner doesn't laugh. He gets up to take a call, shoves an application Pauly's way. He tells him he can fill it out online too, the preferred method. A stuffed raccoon's glass eyes stare at Pauly while he sips from a glass of sparkling water. He leaves the application blank and walks out.

Austin brings a pizza over to the shop for dinner. The box is spread open across Pauly's office desk, on top of used hot dog wrappers covered in dried Coney sauce, unopened bills, and a week's worth of register reports. Detroit-style. Square, crispy deep-dish crust, pepperoni, sausage, and ham.

"Thanks for coughing," Pauly says.

There are postcards from his folks tacked onto the corkboard. Aerial views of white-sand beaches stretching for miles, flamingos standing one-legged, palm trees everywhere. They've been in Bonita Springs for over a decade.

"How was school?" Pauly asks.

"Great. We've been talking about shrinking the city, focusing on building up a condensed area. Creating a kick ass downtown with sidewalk cafés, outdoor concerts, beer gardens. Privately and publicly funded. It's a cool vision. Getting people back into the city to live and work and have fun."

Pauly puts up a finger to speak, takes a second to swallow a big bite. "You know how long I've been hearing about Detroit's comeback, dude? Since 1988, when you were like four."

"A lot of great minds involved on this go-around. Innovators. Entrepreneurs. Doers." Cheese stretches from his hand to clenched teeth.

"I've been thinking more about what you said. About updating the place."

"That's awesome. I can totally help you. You know, the other night I was wondering, what if you rebranded? Revamped the menu."

"There's nothing wrong with the menu."

"I was reading some customer reviews online. I'm not gonna lie to you. Not the greatest." Austin pulls one up on his smart phone that says the mozzarella sticks taste like they're microwaved.

"What's wrong with that?"

"People are more health-conscious these days, Uncle Pauly."

"We do hot dogs. That's what we've always done."

"Do you know they actually have nitrate-free hotdogs now? Veggie dogs. Turkey dogs." Pauly closes his eyes and makes exaggerated nods of the head. "We can be something fresh on the scene if we focus on gourmet dogs. Most restaurants have their own websites too, run promotions on social media."

Pauly laughs. He can't stop laughing. He takes a swig right from a two-liter bottle of root beer.

"We can talk about this later," Austin says. "By the way, good news. I signed a lease today."

"Congrats, my boy."

"I'll be out of your hair next month."

Pauly takes a call from his mom before closing shop. She asks him how things are going.

"Never better, Ma. It's doing me some good having the kid around."

He cleans off his desk as he talks to her, the phone pressed between his ear and shoulder. The "Best of Detroit 1984—WDIV-TV (Channel 4)" bronze plaque hangs crooked above him.

"How's Dad?"

"Good," she says. "He was golfing earlier. Now he's probably drunk at the Tenth Hole."

"As he should be. Tell him not to worry about a thing. We've got it locked down here."

Pauly wipes a table with a wet rag. It's mid-week, and Eighties hasn't stopped humming. Hits from Stevie Wonder—Detroit's famous son—boom from across the way. There's one customer in the corner booth, staring up at the Tigers game. Slick Rick whose forehead is greasy enough to be a bowling lane. He's a sucker for the onion rings.

The door dings when it opens. "Part-Time Lover" rushes in. Pauly looks up and sees Austin.

"What's up, my man?"

"Just thought I'd pop in for a minute."

Outside the door are a group of kids Austin's age huddled together, laughing and flirting. The girls are cute. Smooth skin, sparkly hoodies, and yoga pants. The guys have neatly-trimmed hair and cargo shorts. They grin from ear to ear because they don't know any better, haven't felt life's sting yet.

"Is that your crew?" Pauly says. "Have 'em come in. I'll whip up some curly fries."

Austin stares down at the table, fumbles with his phone.

"Which one's yours?" Pauly says, nodding to the girls. "So I don't put the moves on her."

"They're just friends."

"Right. Sure. Wink wink."

"They're waiting for me. They want to go to this thing."

"What thing?"

"The car thing," Austin says. "Across the street. At Eighties."

Pauly glares at him, dabs his brow with the rag. "Tell me you're kidding. Tell me you're not a turncoat."

"I didn't want you to see me over there and wonder what I was doing."

Darryl peers out from the kitchen. He shakes his head.

"C'mon, Uncle Pauly, it's good for the city."

"Good for the city? It's not good for me."

Austin puts his arm around Pauly, but Pauly shrugs him off. The kid yammers on about the comeback story. About tech startups and urban farming and keeping faith in the American Dream. Pauly tunes him out.

"I should kick you out of my house."

"Where would I go? You know I can't move into my new place until the first of the month."

"Not my problem. Maybe you can move in with the fucking Hot Dog King."

Pauly sees two boys approaching on dirt bikes, heading toward Eighties. "Hold up a second."

They slow down, drag their feet against the pavement.

"You guys are my lucky winners. I've giving free samples to my first group of high school kids tonight."

"We're in eighth grade."

"Close enough."

One of the kids is swimming in a Matthew Stafford jersey. The other has long, scraggly hair and a mouth full of metal like he's Kid Rock's illegitimate teenage son. They each have an ear bud dangling out of one ear. Stafford checks his phone like he's ready to speed-dial 911 if he has to.

"Relax, I'm not Jeffrey Dahmer, for Chrissake. I'm not going to chop you up and stuff you in my freezer."

"Who's Jeffrey Dahmer?"

Pauly has Darryl whip up an order of his Eight Mile High Fries: melted cheddar, sour cream, bacon bits, and jalapeños. Then a couple Coney dogs. He grabs Darryl's pack of cigarettes from the counter and makes an exception on the statewide smoking ban in the name of good marketing. "You guys want a square? Just don't tell your folks."

Pauly paces, chewing on a toothpick. When the food comes out, he watches the boys bite into their hot dogs, listens to the skin snap. He swirls his pop in the Styrofoam cup. The ice rattles.

"So what do you think?" Pauly says. "That's the best Coney dog you've ever had. Killer sauce, am I right?"

The boys look at each other, but don't answer. Stafford shrugs his shoulders.

"Have you been to Eighties?" Pauly says. "Tell me this isn't better than that one by a long shot. Who's the real Hot Dog King, huh? You know it. Spread the word. Go ahead and put that up on Facebook or Tweeter or whatever you young bucks do these days."

Stafford speaks up, his cheeks stuffed. "You don't even have anything fun to do in here, man. No games." He points to Kid Rock's son. "Anyway, he's definitely not going to say this place is better than Eighties. His dad owns it. His dad is the Hot Dog King."

Pauly's mouth drops. "Son of a bitch."

The boys speed off on their bikes. Stafford yells back as they dart across Lafayette: "Thanks for the free food, bro!"

Pauly shuts everything down, locks up. Darryl lights a Kool. They look on at Eighties, still going strong, basking in the glow of its pole sign. Every bulb works, every letter pops. The fans swirling inside haven't been around long enough to collect dust. To earn it.

"You've gotta use a knife and fork to eat his Coney dog," Pauly says. "The sauce is a soup, ya hear me?"

He hands Darryl his paycheck. "I'm gonna try to get the next one to you on time, I promise. Thanks for hanging in there with me, slim."

At home, he sits in his living room recliner with the lights off, drinks vodka straight. He flips through one of Austin's textbooks on the coffee table. He calls his old man. He doesn't answer. Doesn't have voicemail. It just rings. *So I've hit rock bottom, Dad,* he wants to tell them. *Tell me what I'm supposed to do now.*

He lays awake for hours staring at his bedroom ceiling. The kid hasn't come home. In a half-dream, Pauly imagines black and white photographs plastered all over the shop. Its history. Breaking ground. Ribbon cutting. Lines around the block. He thinks about blowing it all up, staring at a blank canvas. What about Coney dogs and apple pie? Coney dogs and barbeque? What could be more American than that? It would be him and the kid. Detroit's dynamic duo. This is America's Comeback City. The Rust Belt Revival. He tosses and turns, listens for the front door to open, wishes it was morning already.

TOYS IN CLOSETS

The camcorder is positioned to show only ToyCollector's delicate hands and the ten Play-Doh Surprise Eggs she's about to uncover for her viewers. Her fingernails are Minnie Mouse manicured. A ukulele strums in the background. She has a glass of lemon water beside her to keep her throat moist.

"Hi friends, ToyCollector here." She knows her voice is a lure. "Today I have ten wonderful surprises for you. Shall we begin?"

She takes the first plastic egg, peels the pink Play-Doh off of it, and twists it open to reveal the toy hidden inside. She brings the toy close to the camcorder, tears at its packaging, makes sure it crinkles plenty because she knows there's no better sound than the unwrapping of a prize. "Let's see what's inside. Can you guess who this is? That's right. It's Hello Kitty Ballerina."

ToyCollector is alone in her high rise condo. From the window, she looks across the Hudson. She hears the neighbors lock their door and chit chat as they walk to the elevator. She wants to shush them. Her Persian cat passes with a Barbie doll in his mouth, pauses to peek his copper eyes into the living room, but knows better than to come near when she's filming.

ToyCollector continues like that—opening eggs, shedding Play-Doh from little surprises, playing with the figurines—for twelve minutes. There's Strawberry Short-cake and Cowgirl Dora, My Little Pony and Peppa Pig.

She stops the recording. It's almost six P.M. and their reservation is for seven-thirty.

"I may be meeting my prince tonight," she says and crosses the plastic fingers of Sofia the First. She uploads the video for her young fans in Asia who must now be rolling out of bed.

They meet in the lounge of Le Bernardin. French hip-hop music is playing. Peter is sipping on a mezcal cocktail. She told him she would be wearing a red and black, rose-patterned evening dress, and he recognizes her immediately. Peter is in a shiny beige sport coat, no tie. He's taller than she expected, and she worries he'll think she's too short. Her heart palpitates. She doesn't know what to do with her hands.

"You're even prettier than in your pictures," he tells her. She looks down, but his words are a haven. "And I like the nails."

They get seated in the main dining room, next to the centerpiece of soaring white orchids. A giant oil painting of foamy ocean waves swishes behind them, the Atlantic or Mediterranean she imagines, perhaps the dawn after an overnight storm.

"I detect an accent, don't I?" Peter says. "Were you born overseas?"

"Ukraine, in a small town. But I've lived here, my Gosh, for over twenty years now."

"Any family with you?"

"None," she says.

They toast to a great evening, clink flutes of sparkling wine. It's always been hard for her to hold eye contact for long. She tells him how her family was poor when she was growing up. Her parents sent her to America to live with her aunt and uncle, since deceased. She finished high school in New York, earned her associates degree from Kingsborough Community College in Brooklyn. She worked various jobs after that, mostly in retail, but she answered phones for a law firm and worked as a bank teller too. Then the toy videos blew up.

The waiter brings them the first course, yellowfin tuna, thinly pounded and laid over a cool slice of foie gras. It's drizzled with extra virgin olive oil, sprinkled with shaved chives. He pours them a 2012 German Riesling.

"Mmm, fantastic." ToyCollector wants to avoid talking about toys, how many she owns, what her videos are like. About toys overflowing from her closets, under the beds, and the kitchen cabinets. Above all, she dreads him asking her the name of her channel or if he can see one of her videos. She's scared men off before. "So tell me more about yourself," she says.

"What do you want to know? Shoot."

ToyCollector was set up with Peter through a millionaire dating service. He's the CEO at a marketing and consulting firm. He tells her he was raised in Iowa. "Hawkeye for life," he says, and she doesn't get it but laughs anyway. When she asks him about his family, he says his parents still live in his childhood home even though he offered to help them buy a new one. He has two kids in college from a previous marriage. He's forty-nine. He says at his age he's okay with full disclosure.

"But I want to hear more about these videos you make," he says. "Almost two billion views. And you're not affiliated with any multichannel network? It's fascinating." He swirls a piece of charred octopus in the sun-dried tomato sauce vierge.

"There's not much to say," she tells him. "I started posting the videos for my nieces in the Ukraine and then other people started watching, liking them."

ToyCollector sinks into the cigar-colored leather chair, dusts her strawberry red lips with the white cloth napkin. Her voice grows quieter, overtaken by table conversations and the clanking of silverware to dishes. Peter leans in closer, turns one ear. "I never sought out to get rich from it," she says. He doesn't pry.

ToyCollector is the third most viewed YouTube channel worldwide. It has advertisements from Fisher Price, Nickelodeon, and Coca-Cola, among others. She's never revealed her real name, though, never shown her face on camera. She suspects Peter may not believe her since she doesn't go on and on about it like some people would. She couldn't possibly have become a millionaire by making videos of herself playing with toys. She must have had a big divorce settlement, a winning lottery ticket, a dead spouse. She doesn't blame him.

After the Parisian tea cakes and coffee, Peter insists on paying. He puts his hand on the bill, making sure she doesn't see it, and she eyes the brownish-gray hairs crawling up the back of his hand, the yellow wristband pedometer slipping out of his sleeve. He says it was a true pleasure, that he had a wonderful night, and walks her to a taxi. "Broadway and eighty-third," she says. He kisses her on the cheek and asks if he can call her. She says yes, of course.

ToyCollector goes for an espresso every morning at the café below her building. She likes that they serve fresh-baked bread and smoked fish. And there is something about going out in the morning and being around people that has always made her feel less lonely, reminded her of home.

Her friend Ruben approaches with a smile stretched beyond its norm. He has gaps between his teeth like a toddler. His head is newly shaven, revealing a jagged scar. Ruben is a server at the café; he was a busboy when she first started frequenting it. He emigrated from Puerto Rico and reminds her of herself. A dreamer. One big idea from a far different life.

"I have some good news, girlfriend," he tells her. "Are you ready? Derrick and I are getting married."

"Oh my gosh, congratulations." She gets up from the wrought iron chair to hug him. The dishware on the table rattles.

"I want you to be there. September fifteenth. Put it in your calendar." Ruben pulls an invitation from his waist apron and hands it to her. They've only ever seen each other in the café. "You can finally meet Derrick. And my little girl. Hopefully."

"You never told me you had a daughter?"

"Yeah, three years old. I had her before, you know. Before Derrick. Long story. Her mom is still pissed at me though, so we'll see if she lets her come to the wedding. I haven't broken the news to her yet."

Ruben excuses himself to wait on another table. ToyCollector inspects the invitation. Two vintage grooms in tux and tails. Pink and brown accents. *Come Celebrate,* it reads. Ruben hustles back with her espresso.

"Yeah, her name is Jazmin. My daughter. How about you, ever married?" he says.

"No, never."

"I find that hard to believe. A gorgeous woman like you."

She laughs. "I'm weird. And I don't trust many people, especially men. I think it got worse when I immigrated here, to protect myself. I was so young."

A gust of wind picks up. *The Wall Street Journal* rolls down the sidewalk. ToyCollector is momentarily distracted by the fragrance of the potted geraniums: lemon, peppermint, nutmeg.

"I would love to get married, though," she says, "have a family, a daughter. I get so lonesome sometimes. And my clock is ticking."

"No, how old are you? Have I ever asked you that?"

"In my thirties. We'll leave it at that."

"You're in the prime of your life."

ToyCollector will be forty in two months. "I went on a date last night. He's a little older than me. Forty-nine, but men can have children at any age, right?"

"Look at you, all giddy." Ruben winks, taps her leg with a menu. "Forty is the new thirty. Invite him to the wedding. Get your man thinking, girlfriend."

Lourdes lays on the double bed she and Jazmin share, lost in *Mi Corazón es Tuyo*, the telenovela she is presently addicted to. A fan blows side to side in the corner of the room. From the open window, she can hear kids hollering under lit street lamps and ambulances squealing. On the television screen, Isabela and Fernando are in his office. She asks him if he's interested in her, and he confesses he is. The two kiss, Isabela's French manicured nails running along the back of his neck, pulling him closer, as Ana spies on them through the crack of the door.

Jazmin is on the floor, watching toy videos on Lourdes's phone, one after another. She's hypnotized by them. The kids Lourdes nannies tell her they love them too, even though their parents don't allow them to watch any television or videos while she's taking care of them.

"Watch, Mami," Jazmin says.

"Shhhh, Mami's tired. Mami needs some down time."

Lourdes runs after three kids all day and commutes an hour each way between the Bronx and Battery Park. The toy videos put her to sleep. Faceless women playing with toys Lourdes can't afford to buy her daughter anyway.

The door buzzes and Lourdes waits to see if her mother will get it. Her mother is in the apartment's kitchenette preparing dinner, arroz con grandules, her speciality. "*¿Puedes abrir la puerta?*" her mother finally says after the second buzz.

"*Sí, mamá, sí.*" She pauses the show and forces herself out of bed. Pots and bowls full of various ingredients are spread out on the kitchenette counter. Ruben is downstairs. She presses the button to let him in, unlocks the front door, and swings it open. She can hear him climbing the stairs. She turns her back and starts walking to the bedroom as he surfaces.

"You're early," Lourdes says. "I haven't even gotten her ready yet."

"Well I was hoping to talk to you for a minute."

"Papi!" Jazmin runs to Ruben, wraps herself around his legs.

"*Mi amor,*" he says and pecks at the top of her head with kisses.

"What do you want to talk about?" Lourdes says. "My show is on. Do we have to talk now, seriously?"

She doesn't make eye contact with him. Her mother doesn't either. Her mother hasn't said two words to him since the separation. She calls him El Diablo when Jazmin isn't around, even though it's been over two years.

Vegetable oil sizzles in the caldero on the stovetop. Lourdes's mother mixes in sofrito and tomato sauce with a wooden spoon. "*Ven aquí,* Jazmin," she says. She lifts Jazmin into the chair and gives her the phone book and a handful of crayon stubs, but Jazmin keeps watching the toy videos on the phone.

Lourdes and Ruben go into her room. She sits on the edge of the bed, atop unmade sheets, and plays her show. Ruben talks over it, over Ana telling Fernando that Isabela is a no good for nothing.

"Derrick and I are getting married," Ruben says.

Lourdes doesn't look at him, keeps staring at the television. Her eyes roll. "Great," she says. "Good for you."

"Hey, I want you and Jaz to be there," he says and touches her arm. "You're my family. I'm barely going to have anyone else there. It would mean a lot to me."

"I don't know how I feel about that. I have to think about it."

"Come on, Lourdes. I love you both." He grins. The same silly grin that melted her when they first met, that made her fall for him. She still can't look at his eyes because they used to be her safety net, her fire escape.

"Let me think about it, okay? I don't know. I have to digest this, for real."

Jazmin runs into the room, waving the phone. Her black ponytail bounces on top of her head. "Can you buy this for me, Mami?" she says. It's the hot pink Hello Kitty Dance Party Limo.

"You know I can't afford that," Lourdes says. "How about your papi over here? Why don't you ask him?"

That night, Lourdes and Jazmin are in bed. The room is hot and sticky, and Jazmin is restless. She kicks the sheets.

Her little toenails scratch at Lourdes's stomach. Her big hair falls over her face. Lourdes still can't believe Ruben found a man before her. *Fucking Ruben*, she thinks. And now he expects her to put everything aside and join in his celebration? *Please. No way in hell.* She grabs her cell phone from the night stand. Its light illuminates the room and Jazmin turns her body toward the wall. Lourdes crafts a text to Ruben: *You've got to be one dumb mofo if you think we're coming to your damn wedding.* She doesn't press "Send."

She wonders about what her life would be like without Jazmin. She could go out with her girls, date, get drunk, have sex again. She misses sex. She feels guilty for thinking like that. Jazmin pops up. "Go to sleep, baby," Lourdes says.

For months, Lourdes's mother has been telling her to get Jazmin a toddler bed. "With what money, mamá?" she asks. Truth is, Lourdes isn't ready to sleep on her own yet.

She tries to distract herself by thinking about *Mi Corazón*. When will Fernando and Ana fall for each other already? How is he going to react when he finds out she's a stripper? Can he save her from that awful life?

Peter's home is in Greenwich, Connecticut, forty miles outside of Manhattan. He and ToyCollector take the Metro-North train there together from Grand Central

Station after he's finished with work. This is her first time there.

She sits in the den, on the mahogany leather sofa, and rubs her fingers against the gold nailheads along the front of the arm. Mounted deer heads surround her. Peter's black and white speckled coonhound sniffs at her feet. The kitchen overlooks the den and Peter is in there, phone pressed between his ear and shoulder, ordering a pizza and peering into the freezer.

"Kind of silly I have a whole house to myself," he had told her over the rumbling of the train on the tracks. "But, after the divorce, I didn't want to end up living in the city, where I work all day. I wanted to have a quiet place where I could get away, go hunting, hiking."

Peter comes into the den with two frosted mugs full of foamy beer. He puts them on coasters atop the dark wood coffee table and lets the dog outside through the sliding glass patio door. Behind the house, there is a pine forest for skyscrapers and wide-open dirt roads for clogged city streets. She imagines what it would be like to live there. To wake up and have coffee with Peter every morning, in the company of trees.

"Did you work today?" Peter says.

"I did. I posted a video of Polly Pocket Color Change Makeover Salon."

"My favorite. Can I see it?"

She stares at her hands, at her flower-pattern finger-nails, and giggles. "I didn't have a lot of toys growing up."

He puts his arm around her and pulls her in. "I'm teasing you," he says. "But you know if you let me do your marketing, I can make you a millionaire. Oh wait, you already are one." They laugh and reach for their mugs.

The closer he gets, the greater her urge to run home and finally corral the boxes of playsets multiplying in every corner, to dispose of the cans of Play-Doh hidden in closets, certainly hardened by now.

"I want to ask you something," she says. "I know we haven't known each other for very long, but I've been invited to a friend's wedding and was wondering if you would be interested in going with me. You can tell me if you think it's weird."

"No, no."

"It's September fifteenth. My friend is marrying another man."

Peter taps his fingers against his blue-jeaned knee. ToyCollector stares at the stone fireplace and scans the photos on the mantel of kids and dogs and graduation gowns. The coonhound howls outside.

"Are you uncomfortable with that kind of thing?" she asks.

"What, you mean two men getting married? No, I have no problem with that. I'm hip. I'm just thinking, September fifteenth. It's the first day of bow hunting season."

"I understand if you can't make it."

"Every year we do this big thing, me and a bunch of guys. It's kind of a tradition."

She looks down into her mug, the foam settling. "I completely understand."

At home, ToyCollector lays on her stomach against the plush carpet, elbows holding up her torso. A glass of zinfandel is beside her. Her Persian watches from the couch. Peter didn't even kiss her goodnight.

She rips open the Disney Princess Ariel and Prince Eric Fairytale Wedding dolls. Ariel's gown is sparkly. She has a purple bouquet and a long, white veil. Eric is in full blue, gold, and white regalia. She uses the *Frozen* Kristoff figurine as the wedding officiant. The camera is not rolling.

"Dearly beloved," she says in a deep voice, "we are gathered here today to join Ariel and Prince Eric in holy matrimony. Ariel, do you take Eric to be your lawfully wedded husband?" Her voice gets higher-pitched. "I do. And Eric, do you take Ariel to be your lawfully wedded wife, to have and to hold. I do. Well then you may now kiss the bride."

Plastic faces press together. ToyCollector plays "Part of Your World" on her iPod. When she's an old woman, she thinks, will her toys bury her? She wipes mascara-tainted tears and gets up to refill her wine glass.

Lourdes pushes the baby in the bucket swing at Rockefeller Park. The Orbit stroller is parked behind her. She keeps an eye on the six-year-old climbing up the plastic yellow slide, the three-year-old clawing through the sand box.

"You never suspected anything?" the other nanny asks.

"Not really," Lourdes says. "Everything happened so fast. We met at a party and he was cool and fun. Sometimes I think I would catch him staring at other guys or being flirty with them when he was drunk, but nothing crazy. We dated for a minute, sort of, and the next thing you know, I was pregnant with Jaz."

"How was the S-E-X?"

"I mean, it was pretty good actually. Better than what I'm getting now."

Jazmin is with her grandmother this morning, either helping her cook lunch or sitting glued to television cartoons. Lourdes watches the McAllister kids four days a week, sometimes a few hours on Saturdays. The rest of her life is spent with Jazmin, except when Ruben comes and takes her off of her hands every couple weeks. Lourdes has been meaning to bring Jazmin to Rockefeller Park, to show her the concrete dog heads spitting water into a trough, to let her ride the kid-pedaled carousel, but she can never get motivated to make the trek on her days off.

"He went to all the doctor's appointments with me," Lourdes says. "Basically moved in with me and my mom, would wake up at night to feed Jaz when she was a baby.

And then when she was like one year old, he told me he thought he might be gay, and that was it."

"Damn. And you're still not over him."

"I mean, it's not like I'm not over him. I'm totally over him. I'm just not over the whole situation. When I see him, when I think about my life now, I still get so angry. I can't help it."

Lourdes and the baby relocate to a shaded bench. Sailboats dot the river in the distance. A camp moves in, more and more kids, their backpacks stacked up against the fence, running under the hippo and elephant sculpture water jets. She spots her two by the climbing nets. "Five minutes, guys," she says. They keep darting across wooden platforms, up and down ladders.

"Yeah, I was supposed to go to school to become an X-ray technician," Lourdes tells her friend.

"You can still do it."

"When? I don't have the time or the energy."

"Girl, you got the time, c'mon. I can't speak to your energy. You can even take online classes now."

"Yeah, we'll see."

"So do you think you'll go to the wedding?"

"I don't know yet."

"Maybe you need to go. He's obviously moved on with his life. It might be good for you to get some closure and move on with yours."

The baby starts crying and Lourdes digs into the diaper bag, pulls out a bottle. She looks for the kids and finds the three-year-old. "Where's your brother?" she asks. The three-year-old shrugs her shoulders.

Lourdes picks up the baby who is still crying. She weaves through kids and parents and other nannies, stomps through the sand pit, gets her feet caked in wet grit. She screams the boy's name. "Do you see your brother anywhere?" she says. She ducks under wooden platforms, rocks the baby, peeks into the gazebo. She finally finds him lying in the red nylon webbing like it's a hammock, hidden by other kids jumping around trampoline-style.

"You almost gave me a heart attack," she says. "Let's go, move it."

The boy slides out. Lourdes says goodbye to her friend. "See you next week," she says. "This is my life, see?"

"It don't have to be, girl."

When Peter calls ToyCollector to meet up for coffee, he has not contacted her in four days. She sits at the café, blowing into a steaming espresso. Her hand rubs the Super Why Princess Presto action figure in her purse.

"He's going to end it with me," she says to Ruben. "I think he wants to do it in person because he's a gentleman."

"How do you know that? C'mon."

"Women know these things. And he hadn't even seen my weird side yet."

"It's not too late. Maybe he needs to, girlfriend."

Peter arrives in blue jeans and a denim shirt. ToyCollector loves that he never looks as wealthy as he is. He leans down and kisses her on the cheek, then scoots the chair out across from her and sits. He doesn't take his sunglasses off, and she wonders if it's strategic.

"So how've you been?" he says.

"Good." She stares at him, nods her head, then looks down into her espresso and begins laughing. "Sorry, this is awkward for some reason."

"Awkward? No."

Ruben comes to the table and stands tall in front of them, hands behind his back, his gap-toothed grin reaching from one side of his face to the other like a string of Christmas lights.

"This is my friend, Ruben," ToyCollector says. "The one who I told you is getting married."

"Yes, Ruben. Congratulations." They shake hands.

"Thank you, sir. What can I get for you?"

"A regular coffee, please."

Ruben hurries back into the shop. Peter takes off his sunglasses and peruses the menu. ToyCollector waits for him to speak. She gazes at the lipstick around her mug's rim. Her heart pounds. She considers telling him she wants to break things off. She doesn't want to be in a relationship, even though she wouldn't mean it.

"Do you want to split a crêpe?" he asks. "Nutella and banana, okay?" She nods. Peter closes the menu and rests his elbows on the table. "I'm sorry I didn't call you sooner. I've been swamped at work."

Ruben returns with the coffee. Peter peels open a creamer cup. Ruben peers at him. "So are you coming to the wedding with my friend here or what?"

"He can't make it," ToyCollector interrupts. "It's the first day of hunting season. Bow hunting?"

"Bow hunting, that's right."

"It's going to be fun," Ruben says. "I bet it'll be more fun than bow hunting. We're going to have Piña Coladas and Samba dancing."

"I do love a good Piña Colada. But, unfortunately, I have to admit I've got two left feet." Peter smiles at ToyCollector. Her hands are cupped around the coffee mug. She shrugs her shoulders.

"The invitation is still open," she says. "It's your decision."

Peter scratches the gray stubble on his chin. He laughs, and ToyCollector starts laughing too. She fans herself with the menu, before he takes it from her. "Oh, what the hell. The season is three months long. The guys can survive without me for one opening day, right, although I'm going to get a lot of crap for this."

"I promise to make it worth your while," she tells him. "I'm going to hold you to that."

Lourdes and the McAllister kids are stuck at home. The rain is coming down in sheets, cascades down the glass of the Juliet balcony. Lourdes watches them from the kitchen. She slips her phone out of her tote bag to send Ruben a text.

The six-year-old is supposed to be practicing his instrument before lunch, but he's racing Hot Wheels across the walnut hardwood of the living room instead. Cars painted in flames crash into the base molding. "Stop that," Lourdes says. "Play your piano." Mrs. McAllister wants the three-year-old to try writing out the alphabet each day, but she's decided to have an imaginary tea party with her dolls. The house rules are pinned to the side of a kitchen cabinet. The routine is held against the fridge by magnets from family vacations to the Cayman Islands and Punta Cana.

There is milk in the bottle warmer. The baby is in the bouncer, hungry, fussing, batting at the dangling blue monkey. Lourdes has been told to use her phone only for emergencies. She often wonders if the McAllisters are monitoring her with hidden cameras. The text is short. Two words and she drops it back into her tote. *We're coming,* is all it reads.

Ruben and Derrick have a morning ceremony at the Brooklyn Botanic Garden, beside manicured shrubs and a koi fish pond. Peter holds ToyCollector's hand as they stroll through the gardens, over wood bridges.

There are fewer than fifty people there, shuffling into the handful of rows of folding chairs. ToyCollector recognizes some of them from the café. She and Peter find a spot in the back. She smiles and waves to Ruben when he looks her way. The wedding procession begins, the flower girl with big black curls walking down the aisle in a pink tutu. Ruben starts to tear, picks her up and kisses her when she makes it to him, mouths "*Mi amor.*" It's his daughter, no doubt. Throughout the ceremony, Peter rubs ToyCollector's back. He puts his hand atop hers during the vows. After the pronouncement and kiss, Ruben raises his arm triumphantly like he's the Statue of Liberty.

The lunch reception is at a little South African restaurant in Fort Greene with sidewalk seating and graffiti splashed against its outside walls. Puerto Rican wedding favors are pinned to guests as they arrive. The mood is festive like they've gathered to watch a World Cup match. African pop music and Nelson Mandela pop art prints, hand-carved animals and tribal drums. There are colorful, mismatched tables pressed together, the grooms' chairs under a chandelier fashioned from old glass Coca-Cola bottles.

ToyCollector and Peter are seated beside some of Derrick's family from Mississippi. She introduces him as her boyfriend, and he doesn't protest. Ruben soon joins them over lamb samosas and champagne cocktails. He grabs ToyCollector's hand.

"Hey, I want you to meet some very important people." They approach the flower girl and a shorter woman ToyCollector presumes is her mother. "This is my daughter, Jazmin, and her beautiful mami, Lourdes."

"What a pleasure to meet you both," ToyCollector says. She leans down to Jazmin who stares at her lips and follows her words. She wonders if her life and Jazmin's have been joined long before this, somewhere in the emptiness of cyberspace. "Your dad has told me all about you. Is it okay if I give you a few gifts?" She turns her attention back at Lourdes. "Would that be okay?"

"Um…I guess, sure."

ToyCollector goes back to her table and returns with two large bags full of boxes wrapped in Disney paper. She promises to bring more next time. Jazmin hops up and down, looks to her mom for reassurance it's really happening, that the gifts are indeed all for her. Lourdes, of course, appears suspicious, and what mother wouldn't be? As if she's thinking, *Hold on, who is this woman again? And why does she want to give all these gifts to my daughter who she doesn't even know?*

"She's my favorite customer at the café," Ruben says. "The sweetest woman you'll ever meet. And you work in the toy industry, don't you?" That seems to soften Lourdes.

"What do you say to her, Jaz?" Lourdes asks.

"Thank you." She peeks inside the bags. "Can I open one now, Mami?"

After lunch, the bar tables are moved back so guests have room to do the salsa and merengue, the Soul Train line and Cha-Cha Slide. ToyCollector and Peter, sweaty and out of breath, take a seat at a corner table.

"So can you see yourself getting married again?" she asks him.

"Absolutely. Although I'd like to see the inside of my partner's home before proposing." ToyCollector covers her face with her hand. "I'm teasing you," he says and rubs her shoulders.

"Okay, well how about this afternoon then, funny man? How does that sound to you?"

The apartment is quiet when Lourdes and Jazmin get home. Lourdes's mother is gone, probably at the Church praying El Diablo doesn't get a hold of them. Jazmin is wailing on the bedroom floor, still in her tutu, gold cross hanging from her neck, black strands of hair stuck across her wet face.

"You can open one," Lourdes says. "But we're going to give the rest of these toys to the Salvation Army. We don't need them. We ain't no charity case."

She throws a medium-sized gift down and it rolls across the carpet. Jazmin chases it like a stray cat after scraps. She tears the paper from the box, ravages it. There is the crinkling of the packaging and Jazmin's smile growing wider with each rip.

"Doc McStuffins, Mami!"

Lourdes stands in front of the closet, slips out of her dress and into a T-shirt and shorts. Jazmin wants more and starts bawling again, throwing herself to the floor. Her screams compete with the voices on the television, with Fernando and Ana and Isabela.

"Fine, you know what, you're right. She gave the toys to you. I don't even know why I'm arguing." Lourdes takes the bags out of her closet, flips them over, and lets the boxes tumble out. "I can't be mad at you."

She sits on the bed and watches Jazmin unwrap princesses and Play-Doh, playsets Jazmin has cried for before in the toy aisles of Target, still others that are unknown. When Jazmin comes to a toy she is unfamiliar with, she pushes it aside and starts opening the next.

"I can't believe it, Mami!"

Lourdes is not sure she's ever seen her happier. "Why don't you at least save some for Christmas or your birthday?" Jazmin shakes her head. "That's not going to happen, is it?"

The floor is littered with glossy bows and shreds of pink paper. Jazmin picks the first toy she wants to play with, the "Doc is In!" Clinic. "Play with me, Mami," she says.

Lourdes flips off the television and slides down onto the floor beside her. She begins taking the pieces out for Jazmin from their plastic baggies. Little dolls and a clinic bed and a reception desk with phone and laptop.

"Mami is going to get a really good job so I can buy you toys like this, okay?" Jazmin nods wildly. "Mami is going to get a job in a big hospital like the one you were born in. The one with all the doctors like Doc McStuffins. Would that be good? Mami might even bring home a handsome doctor for herself."

Jazmin peels stickers from the sticker sheet and places them haphazardly onto the roof of the clinic. Lourdes embraces her, but Jazmin wriggles and bucks to get out of her grasp and play with her toys. Lourdes doesn't let go. She hangs on to her, sways until Jazmin gives in, as if she's tamed a rodeo bull.

ToyCollector and Peter speed up the elevator to the twenty-third floor. She watches the numbers climb, taps her purse against her thighs. There are too many toys to hide.

"Are you sure you still want to see my place? We really don't have to."

Peter looks down at her with a smirk. The elevator bell dings, and the doors part. There is no turning back. When ToyCollector unlocks her condo, her Persian is there waiting. She bends down to rub his face, behind his ears. Toy parts greet them from the kitchen countertops, spread across the sapphire blue granite. The head of a Fairytale Wedding doll pokes out of the hallway closet. She looks to Peter for a reaction.

"So this is where millions are made," he says.

She presses her hand against his chest and reaches to kiss him for the first time. His mouth tastes like guava juice and tequila. She wants to tell him she loves him. "My gosh," she says, "I can't believe you're here. You're actually here."

He kisses her back. Her tongue pierces his mouth like it's a bullseye. They stumble into the living room, faces mashing, teeth colliding. She steps on the Disney Princess Carriage; Peter kicks aside the Hello Kitty Airline Set. Tomorrow, she tells herself, she'll light a match to the toys she doesn't give away or need. She'll put them in a raft and send them down the Hudson.

Peter takes her clothes off, peeling one layer at a time. Her silver shawl drops to the floor. When he undoes her purple silk blouse, the fabric rustles. He unhooks her lace bra, kisses her breasts, makes her skin tingle. The Persian sits on the couch and purrs. As ToyCollector unzips her pencil skirt, she sees Peter spot the camcorder on the end table. "Should we use it?" he says and laughs. "Make a video for us grown-ups?"

She combs her nails through his hair. "Yes," she says, "we should."

She reaches behind the couch to draw the curtains shut. When she turns back, the camcorder is in his palm. He presses the record button, and the red light comes on. It's the first time the camera has seen her face.

"What's your name, beautiful?" he says.

She stares into the lens and offers her God-given one. She lifts her arms behind her head, unclips her hair and shakes it out, offers her flesh and bones.

BLUE

Another black kid is gunned down by a white cop. Fifteen years old. In Chicago this time, seventh district, Englewood. On Jaylen's beat. He's known the cop for years, thinks he recognizes the victim. Jaylen's wife, Yolanda, lays in bed nursing their first child, his smooth brown skin against her breast. He's only been home with them for a couple weeks. On the TV, they watch protests mount. Black Lives Matter. I Can't Breathe. Hands Up, Don't Shoot.

"I have to go," Jaylen says.

"Be careful, baby. I can't wait 'til you can retire and be done with all this."

He buttons up his uniform in the bedroom mirror. Kevlar vest over a light blue shirt, Chicago flag on the right sleeve. Dark blue trousers. *There's no black or white in the police force, only blue.* That's what they say. *Every one of us is blue.* Whenever tragedies like this happen—accidents— whatever people want to call them, he thinks about how it could have been him when he was a kid. This time he imagines even worse. It could be his own son one day. Are they all blue when they go home to their families at night?

"Just come home looking the way you do now," Yolanda says. That's been their mantra since they started dating.

The baby has fallen asleep on her breast. Jaylen knows rough days are ahead. As a police officer. As a black man.

Protesters march down Halsted with arms raised, blocking traffic. Past empty lots, decaying red-brick two-flats, White Castle, and the Family Dollar. Police cameras are perched on light posts like pigeons. The protesters are peaceful, by and large. Most of them are black. Most of the cops are white. That's how it goes. A young man in a black hoodie and glasses stands on the roof of a bus stop, chanting into a megaphone: "Whose streets? Our streets!"

"Hey hey, ho ho, these racist cops have got to go!"

"No justice, no peace, no racist police!"

Some young punks want to give Jaylen a hard time. He can see their breath in the cold air.

"Yo, what up, Uncle Tom motherfucker?"

"You ain't got shit better to do than fuck with us? Take your ass to the North Side and fuck with some white people."

He doesn't say anything, doesn't engage them. *You don't think I feel you?* he wants to scream out. *You don't*

think I've been pulled over for no reason a dozen times myself?
You don't think I have a black son at home?

Multi-colored Christmas string lights outline the occasional apartment window. Protesters march with blue tape over mouths. They carry signs that say "We Want Justice" and "My Color Shouldn't Determine My Destiny" and "Who Polices the Police?" As the streets swell, the tension grows. There are always those people in the crowd with nothing to lose, who could care less about the cause, about being part of something historic. Somewhere, shots are fired. Jaylen just wants to get back home to his wife and baby, and avoid any trouble. Cop cars squawk as they inch down the street, blue flashing lights painting a streak up Halsted.

A Dixon Family Christmas. Jaylen's parents host. There's the big tree in the living room lit up and full of ornaments. The most recent addition is a ceramic black baby poking its head out of a red stocking that reads, "Baby's First Christmas." The women are in the kitchen, talking and laughing and cooking. The baby is with them, being passed around between his grandmas and aunts. His little cousins run into the kitchen, fall to their knees next to his bouncer to look at him and wiggle his feet, before running back out after each other. He's the prince.

Jaylen can smell the honey baked ham and collard greens. There's sweet potato pie and pineapple cake on the dessert table. The men are sitting around the TV, watching basketball. Cavaliers-Heat, Lebron versus D. Wade who grew up on Chicago's South Side not far from where they are tonight.

"What happened with that kid, J?" his uncle Charles asks. "The one who got shot the other day."

"Wrong place, wrong time. Cop gets a call about a robbery at the mini mart. He shows up. Kid has his headphones in, doesn't hear when the cop tells him to get on the ground. Kid reaches in his pocket for his cell phone and that's that."

"Didn't even rob the store. Didn't even have a gun. Same old story."

"How many more years you got, J?" his cousin says.

"Five more. Twenty years of service. Get my pension, start a second career in security."

"Now that's some shit," Uncle Charles says. "Retiring in your forties. Only in America."

Yolanda is already searching for homes. Imagining where she can picture their children being raised when they finally get to move out of the city. She's looking at the South suburbs where other African American families from the city have moved to. Matteson, Richton Park, Homewood. She says she'd feel more comfortable if their kids grew up around other black kids instead of having targets on their backs, the only black kids in a white neighborhood. He wants to tell her that's not how progress is made, not how society changes, but he can't disagree with her logic.

Someone showed Jaylen a map once of Chicago's racial segregation. Blue dots represented whites, green blacks, orange Latinos. He wondered how whites got to be blue? Races radiated out from the city center in bands, like stripes of a rainbow. The South side of the city was all green, the North blue, and the West streaks of green and orange.

"Did you know the cop?" Uncle Charles asks.

"Yeah, I hung out with him a bunch of times. Regular dude. Played basketball with him. Nice guy. Most cops don't wake up thinking they're going to murder someone that day."

"If the kid was white, he'd still be alive."

Jaylen pauses. "Probably."

Jaylen is patrolling his beat. He pulls up next to another squad car. He knows the other cop. Luciano. Lucky, they call him.

"What do you know?" Jaylen says.

"Did you hear about those two cops who got ambushed in New York? Shot execution-style."

"Man, it's ridiculous."

"People want to hate on us. They don't want us to do our jobs." He sips from his coffee and when he says "people," Jaylen wonders if he's implying black people.

"We should all come down with the blue flu. Call in sick one day. Do you know how fast this country would turn into the Wild fuckin' West?"

A group of kids walk past them, puffy coats and dreadlocks hanging out of winter hats. They mumble to each other, their eyes shifting back and forth from the cop cars.

"I'm going to stop arresting people," Lucky says. "Stop giving tickets. Stop busting people slangin' drugs, beating their girlfriends. I'll just show up and collect my paycheck if it's going to be like this."

Jaylen nods. There's so much he wants to say but won't. Jagged, bare tree branches hover over them. "Keep your head up, my brother," Jaylen says. "Be safe out there."

It's New Year's Eve and Jaylen's shift is almost over. He stops at a gas station to get a bottle of Coke so he can stay awake to celebrate with Yolanda, quietly ring in his son's first New Year. When he walks back to his squad car, there's a white dude pissing on the storefront. He has shiny beads hanging over his coat and a black and gold party hat crooked on his head. A dragon tattoo crawls up his neck, breathes fire. He might be nineteen, if that. *Just get home looking the way you did when you left.*

"Hey, c'mon, man," Jaylen says. "Get on home. Get out of here."

"Fuck you, bro. I'm not doing anything. Why you harassing me?" He stares him down, stares through him. He stumbles as he pulls up his jeans.

Jaylen can turn his back, go into the gas station again and buy a lotto ticket, waste a few minutes until the kid wanders off. All he wants to do is get home to his family. The kid is drunk or high, no doubt. He might be harmless. Probably is. Or he might attack the next customer that rolls up, try to rob the store, walk into traffic and kill himself and somebody else. For all Jaylen knows, he might have his mind set on murdering a cop tonight or a black man or, even better, a black cop.

"Get going," Jaylen says. "I'm not going to ask you again." The kid takes his lighter and throws it down. It skips across the pavement to Jaylen's feet.

"All right, that's it. Get on the ground. You're under arrest."

"For what?"

"Disorderly conduct." Jaylen puts his hand on his holster.

"What, are you going to shoot me?"

"When I tell you to get on the ground, you get on the ground."

"Shoot me."

He knows he can. There's no one else around and he'd have every reason to. Part of him wants to. There are no hands up, sure as hell no pleas not to shoot. The kid has a story. Everybody does. But all Jaylen sees in front of him is another fuckin' hillbilly. He wonders what the ripple effect would be if he shot him. Would it change history? *You want to shoot us? How does it feel to have our black cops shooting your white kids? Are you afraid of us now?*

The kid reaches into his pocket. Jaylen is ready to draw his gun and shoot if he has to. The kid pulls out a pack of cigarettes, crumbles it up, whips it down, and kicks it. His face is red. He takes a few steps in Jaylen's direction, then stops. Split-second decisions. Life or death.

"Don't come any closer. I said get on the ground."

"Fuck the police." He starts pacing, chest swelled, hands clenched. "This a free country. I ain't scared of no police." He's ten feet away.

What if I was white? Jaylen thinks. *What if this kid was black?* His discretion. He pulls out his taser instead of his gun. "Last warning." The kid grunts and spits. When he takes another step his way, Jaylen fires it.

The kid's body locks up and he falls to the ground. Jaylen jumps on top of him and cuffs his hands behind his back. "Dude, dude, what are you doing?" the kid yells. Jaylen finds a boot knife on him. There should be a headline in the paper tomorrow, he thinks, but there won't be: "Black Cop Arrests Armed Redneck Instead of Shooting Him Dead." Change happens in singular moments like this, little dots that add up, grow into a sprawling mass.

At home, Jaylen swaddles his son in the CPD blanket, the Chicago flag twisted around his tiny body. Two blue stripes and four six-pointed red stars. There are three white stripes for the backdrop that represent the city's North, West, and South sides. The baby fusses and cries.

There are things Jaylen hopes he doesn't have to tell his son one day. Things his dad told him. Things that may have subconsciously led him to pursue a career as a police officer. *You're a black male. That's two strikes against you. If you get stopped for a traffic violation, use your Sunday school manners. Keep your hands where they can see them. Don't wear a hoodie. Don't slouch. Keep your pants pulled up and the music low. Be polite. No sudden movements. Don't talk back, not ever. I'll repeat that one. Don't talk back, not ever. Don't give them any excuse to kill you.*

Jaylen prays over his son. What else can he do? "Now I lay me down to sleep…"

He prays the world will be a different place when his boy is grown up. The Chicago map re-configured. No black or white. No bands of green or blue.

CATCHING FIRE

It was 1995 and they played *NBA Jam* on their dorm room floor from morning 'til night, fingertips Dorito-stained orange, Reggie Miller catching fire behind the arc and Shawn Kemp shattering backboard glass with boomshaka-laka dunks, and so when he moved in a few doors down, mid-year, from someplace on the East coast that wasn't New York and got piss drunk on his first night and ate a slice of old pizza from the hallway trash and told them their room smelled like wet fuckin' socks before they'd even been introduced, they decided to drop the controllers and follow him wherever he was heading. It was his idea to start an Adventure Man competition. He earned the inaugural fifty points for strolling through the library in nothin' but Superman boxers. Got another quick hundo for proposing to his Ethics prof. They couldn't keep up with him because the only adventures they were willing to do weren't adventurous at all like the time one of 'em ate a spoonful of mayonnaise for a cool twenty-five. And the rest of the year he just racked up points like Chris Mullin with the hot hand: he stole a Pabst Blue Ribbon-blue recliner out of their RA's dorm, talked his girl into having sex in the Rat Lab at Nakamura Hall, marched into Brown Ballroom and did the hokey pokey during the President's remarks at an alumni lunch. After they'd graduated and he hadn't, he'd still call now and again from somewhere in America, drunk on whiskey, but they were always already asleep, alarms set, toothbrushes pre-pasted on bathroom counters, neckties hanging from doorknobs. He'd leave rambling messages that would get cut off mid-sentence wherein they'd only recognize phrases like "fuck yeah, I'm Adventure Man" and "I miss you fuckers" and "you fuckin' pussies" and they'd talk to each other the next day and compare him to those birthday candles you couldn't blow out. When they got the call years later that his car ended up a big ball of fire wrapped around a giant oak on a long stretch of road somewhere between the sun going down and rising back up, they couldn't fight away tears because he was still so young and had his whole life ahead of him. But how they wished they could jump up and dance for him instead, run outside naked and feel blades of grass dig into the soles of their feet.

SAVIOR

July

Hank peered through the window blinds at the honey locust being blown back like a limbo dancer. His folks, watching *Everybody Loves Raymond* reruns from opposite sides of the couch, didn't even notice the lights flicker. He knew if the wind decided to have its way and tear the house from the ground, they'd be swept up without ever realizing what hit.

The village tornado sirens sounded just before the house went dark. "Let's get to the basement," Hank said.

He hovered over his parents, cell phone lighting their way, as they plodded down the steps, one at a time, hands gripping the rail. "Why are you herding us down here like cattle? Let the Lord's will be done already," Mom said.

"Just be careful, Ma."

They took cover under the stairwell, Mom resting atop the box storing the Christmas tree and Dad, eyes shut, holding himself up by a water pipe. They waited there in silence, ears perked, for permission to go back to their lives or some sign the world was indeed coming to an end.

When the worst had passed, Hank crept out into the night. It barely lasted ten minutes, but the storm had rearranged the neighborhood's unblemished county face. Tree limbs were sprawled on lawns like battlefield corpses. The honey locust had been split in two, its better half spread clear across the street. Nelson, the neighbor, stood in his driveway with a flashlight clenched between his teeth, revving up his generator. "I'm guessing we'll be without power for a couple days or so," he said.

"A couple days, huh?" Hank made out his parents pressed against the bay window. "What am I going to do with them? They're going to go nuts without TV."

"This is nothing, man. Count your blessings. I could name you about a hundred worse scenarios that would wipe us all out in a heartbeat. Google it."

The next day, Hank hid in his cubicle and researched end-of-the-world scenarios. He had his back to his cubemate whose fingers were fumbling between Fantasy Baseball and a box of Popeyes chicken. As it turned out, a modest twister had touched down, missing Hank's house by only a few miles. Nelson was right, it could have been worse. And it would be, if Hank believed the hype he was reading on the Net about December 21. It was the last day of a 5,125-year-long cycle in the Mesoamerican Long

Count calendar, which many believed marked the end of the world as Man knew it. There were a multitude of fears: the mysterious Twelfth Planet Nibiru colliding with Earth, alignment of the December solstice sun with the Galactic equator triggering massive earthquakes and other global upheaval, solar storms that would pummel the Earth and decimate power grids.

A help request came in from a partner of the firm. "My fucking computer doesn't work," it read. His cubemate turned to him. "You got this one?"

Hank closed the browser. He pointed his middle finger at the back of his cubemate's office chair as he walked away. He hated the guy. He hated his job, the people he worked for. He hated the fact that he was too afraid to quit.

"What's the problem?" Hank said when he got to the partner's office.

"I told you already, didn't I? My fucking computer doesn't work."

On the desk was a picture of his wife on a giant stallion, decked out in equestrian attire. His bookcase was loaded with bestsellers he'd probably bought at airport gift shops. He had a "2007 Top Accountant" trophy that looked like something he'd been given by his kids for Christmas. Hank ducked under the desk and started playing with the cords. When he gave one a light yank it fell into his palm.

"I don't have time for this shit," the partner said. "Fuckin' technology. Damn computers."

Hank cracked his head on the way up. He plugged the cord in and started the computer. "There we go. Your power cord must've popped out." The partner lifted his gaze from his Blackberry. "And your battery died."

A guy like this, Hank recognized, with all his worldly might, wouldn't have a chance if the universe decided to attack the Earth. That was the thing of it all. As long as the world was intact, this guy could yell at his computer all day long, f'ing this and screwing that, treat hardworking people like dirt, and be considered king. He could go home to his four-car garage and his 1200-thread Egyptian cotton sheets and kick his dog. But if the world got knocked on its ass, he'd be curled up under the wet bar of his 2000-square-foot basement wondering where in hell his housekeeper kept the canned tuna. And guys like Hank, with faces resembling the surface of Mercury but brains that rivaled those at NASA, would be the fixers, the saviors. Guys like Hank would be the seeds of humanity's next great chapter.

Dad's forehead was pressed against the vision screener. Hank had taken him to the DMV to get his license renewed. It was all the old man had left. He couldn't work anymore; didn't have the energy to do house projects. He couldn't even smoke—doctor's orders. But he could still drive himself and Mom to the produce store or post office on weekday mornings if he chose.

"Read line four," the examiner said, a woman close to his age with platinum blonde curls and painted fingernails reaching out like a hawk's talons.

"L, E, P, V..."

The woman shook her head, chin rested in her palm. "No, no, no, no, no. You're missing all sorts of letters. Try the next line." And more head-shaking. "Do you wear glasses?"

"He only wears them to read," Hank interjected.

"Mm hmm. Let's try again."

"B, K, Q, S..."

"That's enough, sir. There's no way I can pass you today. You're going to have to come back and take it again. Get your eyes checked in the meantime."

"Please, ma'am," Hank said. He felt the collective glare of the mob waiting behind them. "He's a good driver, trust me. We've been sitting here for an hour. The fluorescent lights probably got to him."

"Sorry, hon. No can do."

Hank let Dad drive home. His big head hung over the steering wheel. He blew past a stop sign as they weaved out of the strip mall. "They discriminated against me," Dad said, "I can read perfectly fine. I got all those letters right."

"I know, Dad."

"They can't take away my license just because I'm old. You take away a man's license, you take away his dignity. Might as well put me underground."

"You're right, Dad. I know, you're right."

Hank sat under the light bulb in his makeshift basement headquarters, beside a stack of old comics and a case of bottled water. He was working furiously on a new website he'd decided to create—"How to Survive the End of the World." He envisioned it as being a life boat of sorts for people just like him, a modern day ark. The door squeaked open, and Mom hollered down the stairs, "Dinner's ready. Are you coming up?"

"Go ahead without me. I'll come grab something in a bit."

Hank worked on his first post about essential survival items. He'd been doing his homework. Humans only needed about 1500 calories a day to live. Canned goods had a short shelf life, a year tops. The best bet for survivalists was freeze-dried, nitrogen-packed food in #10 heavy-duty lined cans. Those suckers could last thirty years, perhaps more. Unfortunately, they were out of most people's price range, including his. 2500 smackaroos for a one year supply. Yeah, canned goods would have to do: beans, dehydrated potatoes, condensed milk, some fruits and veggies for a little variety.

Hank wasn't convinced 12/21 was doomsday. But if it was, he wanted to be prepared. If another tornado blew through town, only this time down Hank's street, he hoped to be ready. If nuclear holocaust broke out, if there was a terrorist-delivered smallpox attack, if an asteroid struck the Earth (actually predicted to happen in 2036), Hank's plan was to survive. The basement wasn't an ideal bunker, he knew that. An underground blast-proof shelter was preferable, of course. But he figured the basement was at least a decent option—lots of pipes overhead, a fair amount of ductwork.

"As early as December twenty-first, my friends, there may be nothing left," he wrote. "And we'll have to give rise to an entire civilization from scratch." He added to his growing list: windproof matches, bleach, garden seeds, chicken wire, a can opener.

Hank already had one blogger who "liked" his site: Pam Martin. Her profile picture was a selfie apparently using the bathroom mirror. The camera's flash exploded across half her face. Hank clicked on the photo. From what he could tell, she looked to be in her early forties like him. She was fairly attractive. Attractive enough, but for the Kate Gosselin hairdo circa '08. She blogged about coupon clipping—how to be a couponer, coupon lingo, hot links for coupons. Resourceful, Hank appreciated that. She was the kind of woman who'd have a puncher's chance at weathering a plague. He commented on her blog:

"Good stuff, Pam. Any coupons out there for magnesium fire starters or chlorine dioxide water-purification tablets? Lol."

Hank went back to his site and waited for Pam's response. He continued with his post: "There are so many different catastrophic scenarios that something is bound to happen eventually. My hope is this website helps you survive, friends. My hope is this website saves you."

October

Nelson, the neighbor, was a Sales Specialist in Home Depot's Electrical Department. He'd been bugging Hank to stop by one of his Do-It-Yourself workshops. It finally seemed like the right time. He took Dad along. The workshop was titled, "How to Build a Solar Panel." Hank sucked in the sawdust-laden air; it made him feel like a man.

Nelson had a pencil behind his ear, his orange apron covered in grease and metal shavings, plywood and pegboard resting on his construction boots. "Today I'm going to show y'all how to build a solar panel that can deliver about sixty watts of power in bright sunlight. In layman's terms, that's enough to charge your laptop or run a light bulb."

"That's all?" someone said. "How much would it cost me to build enough solar panels to power my whole house?"

"Well, houses vary in size. I'd say anywhere between ten and eighty K."

Four of the seven people there turned around and disappeared into the hardware aisles. What didn't escape Hank was that if the end days arrived, the first thing to go would be power. He figured it was a good idea to brush up on ways to generate it on his own. He'd been reading about solar energy, not to mention wind turbines, diesel generators, and using stationary bikes to juice up batteries.

Nelson knew his stuff. He'd been an electrician in the Army and had helped Hank and his family with some home projects changing outlets and replacing burnt fuses. He dabbled in other trades too, though, like plumbing and flooring. The guy would make a great addition to any survival community.

Nelson screwed the pegboard to the plywood frame. Dad leaned in towards Hank. "Who's this guy again? I know him."

"It's Nelson, Dad." Hank turned and stared at him, confused. "You know Nelson."

"Oh yeah, Nelson." He was silent for a moment. "He's Aunt Pat's friend."

"No, Dad. Nelson's our neighbor. He's lived next door to us for twenty-five years."

"Hmph." He nodded his head. "The neighbor."

Nelson was holding up solar cells and saying something about tabs and polarities and voltage, but Hank lost focus.

He watched his dad who was staring off into the distance. The old man was losing his mind, and Hank didn't know what to do.

The lawn was buried under dead leaves. The basement was slowly being buried by survival gear. There were mouse traps, a hand-powered grain mill, sleeping bags, fishing equipment, shovels, toilet paper, a crossbow. Hank's prized possession was a box of Cuban cigars—Cohibas—that he'd gotten from Dad on his fortieth birthday. There were only eight left because they'd smoked two of them that night. He'd pick the right moment to appreciate them during the end times, when there was reason to celebrate or when all hope was lost or when there was reason to celebrate all hope being lost.

Hank sat on his computer and played with the wording for a Craigslist ad. He was satisfied with the website, but wanted to take it further. He wanted to attract a community of people with various skills and talents who would join together when catastrophe struck. The ad was intended to generate a little buzz. "Recruiting for a St. Louis survival community," he decided on. He kept the exact location secret so as not to be inundated with vagrants when the final days arrived. He already had four followers, although one—Lee—lived in Singapore.

Hank and Pam Martin, in particular, had grown chummy, commenting back and forth on each other's sites, exchanging barbs. They had a lot in common: both lived in St. Louis County, both Virgos, both obsessed with *Buffy the Vampire Slayer*. The relationship evolved into phone conversations and what Hank hoped would be more. From the basement headquarters, he called her. "Hey, I was thinking we could get together for the Eve of 12/21?"

"Yeah, sure," Pam said. "That'd be great. We can call it a 'Doomsday Party.'"

"'Doomsday Party.' I like that. You never know, right?"

"You never know. Are you going to invite the rest of the group?"

"Yeah, I might. I'll probably do that. Except for Lee, of course. We can order some pizzas. You like Imo's? If all hell breaks loose, we won't be having Imo's again anytime soon."

"I love Imo's."

That night, Hank lay in bed thinking about Pam. He fantasized about them becoming lovers when the end of the world arrived, procreating, beginning the next phase of humanity. They would be dirty and sweaty and hardly even have the energy, let alone the privacy, to make love. But they would give in to their carnal desires because they couldn't hold back any longer and because it was good for Man anyway. He'd wanted to make love to her all along really, since the calamity unfolded, but he was too concerned with keeping himself and the other community members alive. This often happened in high-stress, traumatic situations—individuals fell madly in love with each other. Maybe it was the adrenaline or the high cortisol levels. Hank suspected women would be especially prone to falling for the leader. What he would only come to find out after they'd made love, actually over and over again, was that Pam had wanted him from the start too. Even before the disaster, she'd wanted to be the mother of his children.

December

Hank paced with his coat pressed to his chest. He chewed on his fingernails. Mom and Dad were sitting out in the lobby. The doctor was scribbling notes down on a chart. "So you think we're looking at Alzheimer's?" Hank said. "Dementia?"

"Let's see how the blood tests and urinalysis come back. We'll take it from there. Order some brain scans if we have to. Bring in a neurologist."

Hank leaned back against the exam table; the paper crinkled under him. He looked up at the wall covered in diagrams of swollen prostates, osteoporotic hip bones, arthritic joints. The bleakness of it all was offset by a picture of three happy old ladies doing side-to-side twists with exercise balls. "What can I do to help him?" Hank said. "To fix it?"

"Nothing you can do. Unfortunately your dad's getting older. Things start to fall apart a bit with age. Nature's course. Any family around that can help out?"

"No. No one but me."

The doctor pulled out his pen and jotted something onto a script. He handed it to Hank. "Here, this is the info for a good therapist. It might benefit you to talk to someone. This can be a hard thing to go through."

Hank put it in his back pocket and shook the doctor's hand. He thanked him. For what, he wasn't sure. The guy, with his infinite schooling, could run his tests and slap a name to Dad's constellation of symptoms. But he couldn't save him, couldn't freeze him in time or reverse the effects of his aging. That was the thing with geriatric medicine. The doctor could fill his day with back-to-back appointments, old folks complaining about insomnia and back pain, and he could patch them up, push them back out there to fight the good fight. But in the end he couldn't save them no matter what he tried.

Hank's cubemate was playing Tetris on his laptop. He'd just been promoted to Manager. Still, it wasn't a rash decision Hank was making. He'd been contemplating it for months at least. Only now he finally had the nerve to do it. He cleaned out his desk drawer deciding what to throw out and what office supplies he could potentially find alternate survival uses for. A paperclip, for instance, could be used as an emergency fish hook, a splint for minor toe and finger injuries, or a makeshift antenna for small electronics.

His boss called him down to the office. "You wanted to talk to me?"

Hank had been with the company for a decade-plus, but the job was getting more demanding, not less. Fewer employees, longer hours, emails day and night. He was even starting to get grief about taking time off for his dad's appointments. It wouldn't be long before they replaced him with someone younger and cheaper, easier to push around. *Do you have any idea who I am?* he wanted to tell his boss.

"So what do you need?"

"I'm quitting," Hank said. "I'm putting in my two weeks."

"You're quitting? Why would you do that?"

He thought about it for a second. "I don't know. Because I can, I guess."

On the Eve of December 21, the forecast called for mild temperatures and clear skies. Hank was nervous, nonetheless. He didn't even sleep to his alarm. A gamma ray burst, for one, could occur without any warning at all, cooking the atmosphere and destroying the ozone layer. Plus, Hank was anxious to see Pam Martin in person for the first time.

He was in the basement headquarters, setting up Doomsday Party decorations—confetti and streamers, posters of mushroom clouds, R.E.M.'s "It's the End of the World as We Know It" cued up on the stereo—when he got the call.

"Hank? It's Pam."

"Pam. Hey, what's up? Wait 'til you see these 'Party Like There's No To-Maya' shot glasses I picked up. Hilarious."

"Look, Hank, I can't make it over tonight."

"O—kay."

"There's something you should know too. I realize I'm the only female in the community. I don't know how to say this, so I just will. I'm not capable of having children, Hank. I'm infertile. Which, when we're talking about continuing humanity, kind of makes me expendable."

"Yeah, I mean, that's, you know, whatever, I didn't think—." Hank felt embarrassed, like Pam had somehow infiltrated his secret fantasy. He reminded himself, though, they were part of a survival community and, as such, each had a special role. Being the only woman, Pam had obviously assumed hers, although she certainly must have had other useful skills. Hank listened while she explained premature ovarian failure and how it left her barren. How her mom had it too, even though she was lucky enough to pop out a kid first. How it was a black mark on her family she couldn't manage to avoid. Hank told her stuff like that happened with no rhyme or reason. That he had male pattern baldness that could be traced to every male relative on his dad's side dating back to at least the 1800s, though it didn't seem to provide Pam much solace. She sounded like she was about to cry when she said she'd talk to him later. She told him to have fun with the rest of the group, unaware nobody else was coming, and hung up the phone.

Hank spent the night alone in the basement. He polished off a liter of Dr. Pepper and a large All Meat from Imo's on his own. He watched *Rocky 4* on basic cable, commercials and all. He hoped 12/21 didn't mark the end of the world, because it certainly was no way to go out. After the nightly news and the newscasters mocking the notion this would be Earth's last day, Hank made his way up to bed and checked in on his parents. He cracked open their door. Mom was resting on her side, mouth ajar, arm hanging over the bed. Beside her, though, the sheets had been pushed away. Hank stepped into the room, opening his eyes wide. Dad wasn't there. Dad was gone.

He looked around the house—in the bathrooms, kitchens, closets—but his dad was nowhere. He checked the doors. The front was unlocked. Hank ran outside. The neighborhood was illuminated by Christmas decorations. He could make out the glow of the television in Nelson's living room. He considered knocking and asking Nelson to help him. Nelson, the Army Vet, the Man's man, but he decided to keep going on his own. Hank ran down the block and then turned around and headed back to his car. He crept down the quiet streets, passing nativity scenes, inflatable Santas, and plastic reindeers. Finally, in the distance, he saw a figure. It was Dad, near the playground, about three-quarter miles from the house. Hank jumped out and jogged toward him. His dad was in his blue pajamas, his feet bare and white.

"Dad, where are you going? What are you doing out here?"

"I'm going to buy a pack of cigarettes," he said.

When Hank was just a kid, they'd lived in an apartment. There was a convenient store, Hank recalled, his dad would walk to every night to pick up his smokes.

"C'mon, Dad, get in the car." He wrapped his arm around him. "I'm going to take care of you. I've got something for you. Just come on with me."

When they got home, Hank went inside and clomped down to the basement headquarters. He dug through tents and maps and mosquito netting until he found the box of Cohibas he'd tucked away. He took out two and headed back up. He slipped his sneakers over Dad's cold feet and threw his winter coat over his bony shoulders. They sat outside on the front stoop, and Hank gave the cigars a light, Dad's first.

"Nothing like a good Cohiba, eh Pop?"

He nodded. "Now we just need a little cognac."

What was left of the honey locust hung over them, its branches reaching down like they were threatening to scoop Hank and Dad up, like they were planning an abduction. Hank drew in a puff of smoke and held it for a minute. He savored the taste—its woody flavor, a hint of vanilla—before opening his lips and letting it out. "Watch this, Dad," he said. Hank blew smoke rings at the sky, out to space. He blew them at the giant black holes out there waiting to swallow Planet Earth, at the asteroids preparing to slice through Earth's atmosphere. He blew smoke rings, small ones then bigger ones, at the great unknown inevitably on its way.

ACKNOWLEDGMENTS

Thank you to my wonderful wife for her encouragement, patience, and honesty; our kids, who are my muses, my inspiration; the rest of my family for their enthusiasm, especially my parents, who immigrated to America from Greece, and my brother, the real writer in the family; Dean Kastle, for kindly and passionately reading and editing each story in this collection before it saw the light of day; Leesa Cross-Smith for her constant support, wisdom, and mentorship; several great writers, editors, and artists who have inspired and helped me along the way, including Ben Tanzer, Sara Lippmann, Shawn Syms, Troy Palmer, James Yates, Apollo Papafrangou, Jeff Stark, Ilan Mochari, and Jerry Brennan; Greg and the good people at Tailwinds Press for making this book a reality; and the literary journals and anthologies that published earlier versions of stories from this collection.

The following stories have appeared in the following journals:

"Ain't Like the Movies" — *Necessary Fiction*
"To Abdo, with Love" — *jmww* (reprinted in *Bully: A Collection of Stories* (KY Story, 2015))
"Kinda Sorta American Dream" — *Little Fiction*
"It Takes a Village" — *Prick of the Spindle*
"Hold On" — *Hobart*
"Sixteen Hundred Closest Friends" — *Xenith* (reprinted in *Friend.Follow.Text. #storiesFromLivingOn-line* (Enfield & Wizenty, 2013))
"Red Clay" — *Eunoia Review*
"Kingdom Come" — *ken*again*
"Catching Fire" — *WhiskeyPaper*
"Savior" — *Bluestem Magazine*

ABOUT THE AUTHOR

STEVE KARAS lives in Chicago with his wife and two kids. His stories have appeared in the short-fiction anthologies *Friend. Follow. Text.* *#storiesFromLivingOnline* (Enfield & Wizenty, 2013) and *Bully* (KY Story, 2015), as well as literary journals like *Necessary Fiction*, *jmww*, *Hobart*, *WhiskeyPaper*, and *Little Fiction*. He has a chapbook forthcoming from WhiskeyPaper Press in 2016. Steve can be found online at steve-karas.com.